Jonah and the Last Great Dragon

Legend of the
Heart Eaters

monty

To Albert,

Best wishes,

M. E. Holley

Jonah and the Last Great Dragon

Legend of the Heart Eaters

M E Holley

OUR STREET
BOOKS

Winchester, UK
Washington, USA

First published by Our Street Books, 2012
Our Street Books is an imprint of John Hunt Publishing Ltd., Laurel House, Station Approach,
Alresford, Hants, SO24 9JH, UK
office1@jhpbooks.net
www.johnhuntpublishing.com
www.ourstreet-books.com

For distributor details and how to order please visit the 'Ordering' section on our website.

ISBN: 978 1 78099 541 0

A CIP catalogue record for this book is available from the British Library.

Design: Stuart Davies

Printed and bound by CPI Group (UK) Ltd, Croydon, CR0 4YY

We operate a distinctive and ethical publishing philosophy in all
areas of our business, from our global network of authors to
production and worldwide distribution.

CONTENTS

To Toby Warren

Because he's special

Chapter 1

WATCHERS ON THE HILL

As the sun began to rise, a hooded figure slipped through the trees to the edge of the wood. For a few moments it looked up and down the little valley, then turned and beckoned. The undergrowth rustled as a large, shaggy animal slunk through and came to stand beside the silent form. It sniffed the air, staring down at two farms nestled near the crooked little lane. There was a faint sound from the farmyard directly below. The watchers turned their heads sharply. A boy was opening the yard gate and coming into the field. The being in the hooded robe nodded.

Jonah Drake shivered in the cool air as he looked around the steep meadow. The land felt mysterious in the early morning light, as if the woods were hiding secrets. He gazed up at the line of trees crowning the ridge. The lower branches of the beeches above him trembled. Idly, he wondered why they were moving, when the rest of the woodland trees were as still as cardboard cut-outs.

In fact, the stillness was somehow alarming. It felt as if the misty valley was holding its breath, waiting for something to happen. Jonah had the oddest feeling that he was being watched. The hair rose on the back of his neck and he looked round sharply. There seemed to be a sudden movement at the top of the hill but when he stared at the woods, the trees were motionless. Jonah took a deep breath, shook his head and told himself not to be such an idiot. What could possibly hurt him here?

The long meadow grass had soaked the bottoms of his jeans. He bent down to roll them up and saw, out of the corner of his eye, another flicker of movement up in the trees to his right. Jonah straightened up and gazed at the ridge above him. There was no breeze; the branches were absolutely still. For a moment or two, nothing stirred. And then, yes. Something *was* slipping through the beeches. Jonah stiffened, and then remembered his uncle telling him there were deer in the valley. He grinned with relief. There must be a few in the woods! Perhaps they would come down to feed.

A bird called and another answered from the other side of the lane. The sun was getting higher now. Jonah noticed a buzzard hovering above the ridge on the other side and strained to hear its thin, mewing cry. He paused, listening intently. And then, apart from the buzzard's call, he realised he could hear another sound coming from the direction of the woods.

He stopped and turned, puzzled by the noise. There it was again. He wasn't sure what he was hearing. It was a bit like a low growl. Jonah stood still, hardly breathing, and strained his ears. For a moment, he couldn't hear anything and then it came again, nearer this time. A low, menacing rumble. Jonah turned cautiously to look back the way he had come. The noise stopped.

The silence held for a long moment while Jonah looked wildly around. Then, behind and above him, something crashed in the undergrowth. The bushes rustled, and an animal leaped out of the tree-cover some distance away and stood staring down at him. Jonah froze. The huge creature standing stiffly on the hillside was no deer. He supposed it was a dog but he'd never seen one like it before. It was nearly as big as a pony, with a very pointed muzzle and a rough, dark coat. Its forefoot was lifted slightly, ready to spring. As Jonah stared at it, the dog turned back its upper lip and snarled ferociously. The rumbling growl from deep in its throat carried down the valley. Jonah could feel his legs shaking. It seemed obvious that as soon as he moved, it would go for him.

He swallowed hard and tried to think. He wasn't sure he could get back to the farmyard before the brute caught up with him. The slope was steep just here. If he sprinted, it would be easy to trip and lose his footing. Then the dog would be on him in seconds. Cautiously, he turned his head a fraction to estimate the distance and instantly realised he had made a mistake. The dog launched itself down the hill.

Jonah turned and fled. He pelted diagonally across the gentler slope, making towards the lane. He didn't dare look round to see how quickly the animal was gaining on him. He knew he was going away from the farm but he could run faster in this direction. His foot caught on a tussock of grass. He stumbled, flailing his arms, but managed to right himself. He pounded on, slipping and sliding on the wet grass. His heart hammered against his ribs.

He had a stitch in his side and he was gasping for breath, but he pushed himself on. It wasn't far to the next farm up the valley now. He could see the roofs of the farm buildings over the top of the long hedge bordering the meadow. At first, he couldn't see how to get through. His eyes darted wildly along the hedge and then, as he ran down the slope towards the valley lane, he saw a stile.

Jonah's legs felt like lead weights but fear forced him across the last few yards of the field. At any moment he expected the dog's awful snarl, as it snapped at his back. He threw himself over the stile, flew up the lane and swerved through the farm gate, making for the house at the end of the drive. The gravel crunched underfoot as he ran, heaving for breath. A barn stood on the left of the track. Just as he realised that his legs wouldn't go much farther, there was a shout.

'Hey! Over here!' A girl was standing at the open door of the barn. Jonah lurched towards her but then his energy seemed to drain away. He leaned over, one hand on the barn wall, gasping. A woman came to the door.

'Erin?'

'Quick, Mam, help me get him inside.'

The woman took one look at Jonah and reached for his elbow.

Together they half-lifted, half-dragged him into the barn. Jonah, his fair hair flopping over his eyes, bent double and clutched at his side. His chest was heaving and he couldn't swallow because his mouth was so dry.

The girl's words tumbled out in a rush. 'It was awful, Mam. I haven't seen it round here before. It just really went for him and…'

'Tell me in a minute, love.' The woman looked at Jonah with concern. 'Let's get you up to the house, *cariad*. We'll finish in here later. You need a drink.'

Chapter 2

GILFACH FARM

Jonah walked up to the farmhouse on wobbly legs that still seemed as if they didn't quite belong to him. The girl kept craning her head to look for the dog on the hillside. In the big kitchen Jonah dropped into a chair thankfully, while her mother poured him a glass of water.

'Would you like a cup of tea? Or some juice?' the woman asked kindly.

'No, this is fine. Thank you.' His voice came out in a croak.

She turned to her daughter. 'Whatever happened, Erin? Was someone after him?'

'Not *someone*, no. It was an animal. I saw it up on the hill, right over behind Maesglas, and then it went for him. But I don't know where it's gone now. I couldn't see. The hedge is too high.'

Her mother looked puzzled. 'What do you mean – an animal? A dog, is it?'

Erin shook her head and shuddered. 'Not an ordinary dog. It was awful. It was so big! A real brute.' She looked at Jonah. 'Do you know what it was?'

'No,' Jonah said. 'I've never seen one like that before.' He screwed up his face. 'If it lives round here, I'm going to have a great summer. *Not.*' He flushed, feeling slightly embarrassed. 'I won't want to go out!'

'Nor me.' Erin shuddered.

'We're going to have to find out who that thing belongs to,' said her mother. 'We can't have a dog like that running loose, attacking livestock, let alone people. Think of the damage it could do. You could have been badly hurt.'

Erin sat down at the table too, her dark eyes alight with

curiosity. Her mother had been firm: 'Let the boy recover, Erin, before you swamp him with questions.'

Erin grinned at Jonah conspiratorially but all she said was, 'I'm Erin Morgan. This is my mam, Gwen.'

Jonah felt much better. He got up and put the empty glass on the draining board. 'Thanks, Mrs Morgan. I'm OK now. Thanks for helping me. I'd better be getting back.' He tried not to show how scared he was of walking along the lane to the farm. 'My aunt's going to start worrying when she finds my room empty. She didn't know I got up so early.'

'Your aunt? Oh, I know who you *are*!' Erin's face lit up. 'You're Jonah, aren't you?' She turned to her mother. 'You know who he is, don't you?'

'Well, I don't think I've seen—'

'Oh, Mam! This is *Jonah*.' Her mother looked puzzled. 'Mam, he's Claire Parry's nephew. He's staying at Maesglas. Aren't you?'

He nodded, smiling. 'Yes, that's right.'

Mrs Morgan's face cleared. 'Oh, of course. I remember now. Your Uncle Bryn told my husband you were coming down this summer. But he said you weren't coming until mid-August.'

Jonah smiled. 'Well, I wasn't, at first. And my parents were supposed to be coming to stay for a couple of weeks, as well. But they were offered this contract. It's for seven weeks, running training programmes in a big company in Saudi Arabia. It was just too good to miss. They didn't think I'd have much of a summer if I went with them – you know, just stuck in a compound with no one to hang out with – so I've come down to spend the whole summer with Claire and Bryn.'

'Well, that *is* nice,' said Mrs Morgan. 'We should have met you and your parents in January, you know, if we could have found someone to look after the farm. Bryn asked us to the wedding. We were so sorry we couldn't come up to Lancaster.'

Erin had a huge smile. 'Are you really here all summer? Oh, that'll be just great! I couldn't believe it when Dad said you were going to be at Maesglas for a bit in August. And he said you were my age, too. At least he thought you were. You are about my age, aren't you?' A torrent of words poured out. 'There's hardly ever anyone around to do things with. Do you ride? You can borrow one of our ponies, if you do, and Dad's got an old bike you can borrow. Jonah can have it, can't he, Mam?'

Mrs Morgan threw up her hands. 'Heavens, Erin, let the poor boy alone, can't you? He might be looking forward to a nice quiet time on the farm with the Parrys. Not racketing round the valley with a girl who can't ever stop talking!'

Erin grimaced. 'I know! I always talk too much.' She looked at her mother and Jonah, who were laughing. 'Well, it comes of being a deprived child. Stuck in the middle of the Radnor Forest. That's the trouble with living out here: there's nobody my age, for miles. So when there *is* someone here, I have to make up for it.'

Jonah grinned. He began to think the summer might be good fun.

'I'd better go, Mrs Morgan. Thank you very much.'

'Oh, drop the 'Mrs Morgan', *cariad*. We're not very formal in the valley. You call me Gwen. Everyone does.'

Erin jumped up. 'But what about the dog? It might be hanging around. You can't walk home.'

'I'll be OK,' Jonah said, trying to sound more confident than he felt.

'It's all right,' said her mother. 'I'll give Jonah a lift down the lane. I've got to pop to Knighton for a few groceries, anyway. It won't hurt to go nice and early. Finish feeding the hens for me, dear, would you? Tell Dad I won't be long and, whatever you do, watch out for that dog. We don't want that thing near the farm.'

Jonah climbed into the battered old Land Rover. As Mrs Morgan drove out of the farmyard and turned into the lane, he scanned the hillside anxiously. There was no sign of the dog and he began to relax. Just before Maesglas Farm, Mrs Morgan started to signal a left turn.

'Oh, don't bother to turn down the drive,' Jonah said. 'I'll be fine now.'

'Are you sure?'

'Yes, really. It's only a few yards to the house. Thanks for the lift.'

'You're welcome, dear. We'll be in touch. Say hello to Bryn and Claire for me, won't you?'

Jonah got down and waved as Mrs Morgan drove away. Just before he reached the farmyard, he looked up at the hillside and thought he saw movement. He squinted. Was there someone up in the trees? For a moment, Jonah thought he glimpsed somebody wearing a hood but he couldn't be sure. It could have been a trick of the light.

He looked along the ridge and caught his breath. Oh, no! Just below the woods at the top of the hill, the dog was standing on watch. Jonah halted at once and stood absolutely still. He didn't dare to keep walking, in case it noticed him. For a few seconds, the brute turned its head from side to side, sniffing the air. Then it seemed to catch a scent and slowly turned its head. Its eyes locked on to Jonah, boring into him like needles. In that instant, he knew the dog had been searching for him. Terrified, he dashed towards the house.

Chapter 3

LUNCH AT GILFACH

Breakfast was nearly over at Maesglas Farm when the kitchen telephone rang. Claire got up to answer it.

'It's Gwen,' she said, turning to Jonah. 'She wants to know whether you would like to have lunch with them. Shall I tell her *Yes*?'

Jonah tried to swallow a big mouthful of bacon and tomatoes. He was just about to nod, when he remembered something.

'Bryn,' he mumbled, chewing, 'are you still going to clean out the hay-barn today? Because I said I'd help.'

Bryn shook his head. 'After all that travelling yesterday? *And* being chased this morning? You need to relax.' He smiled at Jonah. 'No, you go and have a look round today. Explore the valley and enjoy yourself. But be careful, mind.'

Later, Claire had driven him up the lane. 'It's no bother to take you. I don't want you running the risk of meeting that dog when you're alone,' she said. 'You needn't look like that. You don't have to feel ashamed of being scared. If I'd been in your shoes, I'd have been terrified.'

Secretly, Jonah was relieved that he didn't have to walk to the Morgans' farm by himself.

They lazed around in the garden at Gilfach after lunch, playing with the litter of black and white collie puppies, which were nearly old enough to go to their new homes.

'I'll miss you so much, won't I?' Erin crooned, cuddling a sleepy bundle of fur. Then she put the puppy gently on the grass and jumped up.

'Do you want to go and explore a bit? Get to know the valley?'

She studied Jonah. 'Are you OK about that? After what happened this morning, I mean.'

'Yeah. It's cool.' But he still felt nervous and hoped it didn't show.

'I'll just let Mam know we're going out.'

Erin ran indoors and came back smiling. 'She says it's all right for us to go, so long as we aren't too far from the farm and I take this.' She held up her smartphone. 'If we see the dog again, we're to ring. Then Dad will get his shotgun and come to find us. He'll soon see the thing off!'

They scrambled up the steep meadow on the other side of the road from Gilfach Farm to wander along the ridge, looking across at the dense tree-cover on the hills behind their farms. From up here they could see Bryn's farm snuggling into the valley. Jonah could not help peering at the woods to see whether the monstrous dog was still around.

'Jonah? Jonah!' He realised Erin was laughing at him. 'You're miles away!'

'Sorry. I was just thinking—' Jonah turned abruptly to Erin. 'If I tell you something, will you keep it to yourself?'

She nodded eagerly.

'Promise?'

'Promise. Cross my heart and hope to die.'

'It's just that it sounds crazy. It's about this morning.'

Erin had flopped down on the ground, her dark eyes alight with interest. 'What? The dog, you mean?'

'Ye-es,' he said slowly. 'Except—'

She sat up. 'Except what? Go on.'

'Except it looked – well, before you say anything, I'm sure it wasn't a German Shepherd or anything like that. It was bigger, wilder looking, and it just didn't look like a Shepherd,' he finished lamely. He reddened, feeling embarrassed. 'I mean, if I didn't know wolves are extinct in Britain, I'd have thought that's what I saw. A really big wolf.'

For a moment they stared at each other. Erin's mouth dropped open. 'But you *do* think that's what it is, don't you? That's incredible!' She shook her head. 'Look, Jonah, it's not that I don't believe you, it's just – well, I'd have to see it again myself, closer up.'

'What would you do if we did see it?'

'Why? Is it there again? Where?' She was staring apprehensively at the woods.

'No, sorry, I didn't mean that. It's just that I wondered what we would do, if we *did* see it again.'

Erin was still gazing down at the woods. 'Let's just hope we don't,' she said slowly. Then she shook her head, as if to clear her mind, and gave Jonah a sideways glance. 'If we *did* see it, we could put a spell on it!'

'Oh, yeah? Like you know one!'

'I do, as a matter of fact. Better show some respect, boyo, or I might put a spell on *you*!'

Jonah chuckled. 'Like what?' He thought for a moment and then, grinning, chanted: '*Abracadabra, Jonah Drake, begone from here. Go jump in the lake.*'

Erin rounded on him. 'You can put that grin on the other side of your face, Master Jonah Clever Clogs Drake, because I *do* know a real spell. See the little church down there?' She pointed to where Jonah could just see a small square tower poking above trees. 'That's St Michael's, and there's an Abracadabra spell on the wall inside.'

'Really? In a *church*?' Jonah could hardly believe it. 'Do you know the spell?'

Erin nodded.

'Say it then. Go on.'

She rolled her eyes. 'Honestly, Jonah, it's a *real* spell. I can't go saying it out loud. It's supposed to be very powerful. Mam says not to mess with things you don't understand. You don't know what might happen. But I do know the spell was used to free a girl from possession by demons. Her name was Elizabeth Lloyd.'

'Wow! When?'

'Well, a long time ago. About 1700, I think. But that doesn't matter. You know it's a proper spell that really works, if people had it put *inside* the church!'

'Can we go down and see it?'

Erin shook her head. 'Not today we can't. The church will be locked. It's only open once a month for the Sunday afternoon service. We could go then, if you like.'

'They only have a service once a month?'

Erin spread her arms wide and whirled around, her dark curls flying. 'Look around you. See the size of the congregation?'

Jonah laughed and gazed down at the valley, where he could see a couple of rooftops near the church and just two or three houses tucked amongst the woods and meadows.

'Yes, I see what you mean. Not exactly a big village, is it? I'd still like to go down to the church, though.'

'OK.' Erin was off, leaping down the hillside and Jonah breathlessly scrambled after her. She stopped suddenly so that Jonah, who could not stop his legs in time, ran into her, and they had to grab each other so that they didn't fall over. Hanging on to Jonah's arm to steady herself, Erin pointed beyond the church.

'Look, can you see that?'

'What?' Jonah, frowning, stared towards the church, but could not see anything out of the ordinary. 'I can't see anything.'

'Yes, look.' Erin turned Jonah's shoulders so that he could look along her outstretched arm. 'Look over to the left of the churchyard.'

Above the dark line of the trees, a thin plume of smoke was rising, not steadily like smoke drifting upwards from a bonfire, but in spurts, as if someone was using a bellows.

Jonah nodded. 'I see it now. Why is it doing that? Coming up in little puffs, I mean.'

Erin was biting her lip as she stared at the smoke. 'I don't know. I can't think what it could be. If it's coming from the woods, it wouldn't be a farmer burning rubbish, would it? I don't like this, Jonah. It might be a forest fire.'

'Come on.' Jonah was excited. The wolf dog slipped from his mind. 'I think we ought to find out what it is.'

Chapter 4

SMOKE IN THE FOREST

They slithered on down the hillside towards the lane as fast as they could, sometimes sliding down where it was steep, and then running as they neared the bottom, where the hill dropped gently towards the road. Erin dropped onto the grass, laughing, while Jonah, panting, was bending over with his hands on his knees.

'Do you think some idiot has dropped a cigarette end and the grass has caught?' he gasped.

Erin grew serious again. 'Well, that's what I'm scared of. When it's dry like this, the bushes can go up like tinder. It's odd, though, the way the smoke is coming up, bit by bit.'

'Quick, then. Let's go and see,' Jonah said.

They hurried up the steep lane between the two stone cottages that lay on either side of the road by the church gate. At the end of the churchyard wall, there was a metal farm gate opening into a small hilly field, running steeply down to thick woodland. Now they could see the puffs of pale grey smoke again, rising high in the air.

'It doesn't smell bad,' said Erin, stopping to sniff the air, 'so they aren't burning old tyres or anything.'

'And it's not spreading,' Jonah said. 'The smoke is just going straight up in a thin stream, look. Come on, let's get a move on.'

They ran along the top of the sloping field until they were level with the plume of smoke and then Jonah saw that there was a brook at the bottom of the hill, dividing the meadow from the woods.

'How do we get across? Where's the bridge?'

'Oh, who's a little townie, then? We don't have *bridges* out here.' Erin grinned as she sat down to pull off her sandals. 'Come on. Take your trainers off. It's not deep. We can wade across.'

She ran down the slope, sat on the bank and slid carefully into the eddying water. 'Ooh, it's cold,' she called, giggling. Jonah rolled his jeans as high as he could and lowered one foot into the stream.

'Wow. It's freezing,' he gasped, stepping down into the swirling current and feeling for a foothold on the slippery mud at the bottom.

'Don't leave your shoes. You won't be able to walk through the undergrowth without them.'

They crossed the brook carefully, up to their knees in water, trying not to lose their footing on the sharp pebbles and mud.

'It's not going to be easy walking through here,' Erin said. They wiped their feet as well as they could on the grass and put their shoes back on. 'And we won't be able to see much; we'll just have to follow the smell of burning.'

The larches and pines closed around them as they plunged into the woods. Twigs crunched beneath their feet and sunlight occasionally flashed through the leaves, as the children ducked under branches and followed the smoky smell.

'Here it is!' cried Jonah, holding a prickly branch aside for Erin. 'I can see it now.'

They moved out from the dappled light under the trees into a clearing. Thick smoke was eddying upwards through winking shafts of sunlight. They both stopped and stared, coughing as the smoke caught at their throats. Instead of the bonfire they expected, there was an enormous fissure in the ground, running through the forest, as if the earth was cracking apart. Several trees were leaning over with their roots high in the air, as if a giant had come through and pushed them clumsily aside. Out of the cleft came puffs of smoke, and sometimes a tongue of flame leaped into the air.

'What is it?' Jonah asked.

Erin was wrinkling her forehead. 'Haven't a clue,' she said.

'But there's something terribly wrong.' She turned to Jonah, clutching his sleeve. 'Oh, you don't think it could be the beginning of – well, a volcano, do you?'

He shook his head, frowning 'We haven't got volcanoes in Britain.'

'But that doesn't mean we never will. What about those plates in the Earth's surface that move and form mountains? We've just done those in Geography. Do you think that could be what's happening?' asked Erin, wide-eyed.

'I dunno. It's weird.'

Jonah picked his way over the uneven ground towards the giant fissure and craned his neck to peer down into the smoke billowing from the crack.

'Jonah, don't! If you slip, you could get killed.' Erin was panicking.

'It's OK. I'm being careful.'

'But if you can't see properly because of this smoke—' She broke off, coughing.

The smoke made Jonah's eyes water. 'All right. I'm coming back now.' As he moved away, he felt something suddenly catch his leg. He tried to pull away but a creeper, or something like it, tightened round his ankle. He yelled in alarm as his foot was jerked from under him and he felt himself being pulled over the rough ground towards the smoking pit. Erin screamed and then threw herself flat on the ground, crawling towards him.

Jonah scrabbled at the earth to try to get a hold on something. He kicked out in terror with his free foot, as he felt himself slipping towards the edge of the chasm. The intense heat began to sear his skin. He grabbed at a tree root protruding from the hard earth and hung on. He felt Erin beside him and then her hands were round his arm. She hung on fiercely, her fingers digging into his flesh; Jonah felt as if he was being ripped in two. Then, as suddenly as it had begun, his foot was free, and he was able to scramble backwards. He fell against Erin and they both lay on the bare earth, trembling. After a moment or two, they shakily got to their feet.

Erin was leaning with one hand against a tree trunk, coughing in the smoke and struggling to get her breath. Jonah patted her shoulder.

'Thanks,' he said. 'If it hadn't been for you —' He faltered and felt a lump grow in his throat. *I might have been killed,* he thought. He took a deep breath, which made him start coughing, and went on. 'What happened? I just couldn't get my foot free. It felt like something grabbing me. Did I get caught up in some ivy?'

Erin was staring at him. She looked afraid. 'No,' she said in a wobbly voice. 'But – you won't believe me.' She was gazing at him, almost pleadingly.

'I will,' he said.

'Promise you won't say I'm mad.'

'I won't. Really. Cross my heart and all that.'

'Jonah,' her voice dropped to a frightened whisper, 'I think it was a hand. I do! Honestly.'

He stared at her. A cold prickling feeling crept up his spine.

'I saw fingers,' she said. 'All long and greyish, with horrible horny fingernails. I swear I did. I know people would say you got your foot tangled in brambles or something. But you didn't. You were being *pulled along*! Oh, please say you believe me.' She looked anxious. 'Please don't think I'm a freak!'

Jonah shook his head. 'I don't,' he said. 'To be honest, it didn't feel much like ivy. What I felt round my leg – well – it actually could have been fingers!'

They gazed at each other in horror and then, yelling, 'Let's get out of here!' they plunged through the undergrowth towards the little stream.

Chapter 5

MEETING MR GOLDING

They scrambled up the bank into the meadow. There were bleeding scratches on their arms and necks, where twigs had scraped them as they ran. Erin's shirt had ripped on a thorn and Jonah had smears of red-brown earth all down his back. Panting and exhausted, they looked at each other and then Jonah began to grin. 'Do you think we might get A for Imagination?'

Erin took a deep breath and looked around the sunny, perfectly normal meadow. She smiled ruefully. 'Perhaps B plus.'

Jonah gave her a sideways grin. 'Oh! Oh! The Ivy-man cometh with his horrible horny hands. Waaah!'

Erin started to giggle. Jonah, waggling his fingers, made a grab for her and chased her across the slope. She gave up, out of breath, and they flung themselves down on the grass, laughing. But another column of smoke shot upwards, making them feel anxious again, and they started up the hill towards the lane.

'Do you think we ought to go and get your father? Or shall we go to one of the cottages to tell someone about the fire? That would be quicker,' Jonah was saying, when Erin exclaimed, 'Look, there is someone coming already.'

At the far edge of the meadow, a man had just come through the gate by the church and was coming down the grassy slope towards them. He was tall and young-looking, wearing khaki chinos and a dark green polo shirt, and the sun lit his blond, curly hair. He gave them a wave as he came nearer.

'Who's that?' Jonah whispered.

'I don't know,' Erin replied, puzzled. 'He's not from round here.'

The man smiled as he came down the slope towards them.

'Hello,' he said. 'I *thought* I saw movement in the woods. Did you see the smoke?'

Jonah nodded. 'Yes, we were up on the hill behind the church,' he began, but Erin cut in.

'Excuse me,' she said, looking at the stranger with a slight frown. 'Are you on holiday here?'

The man shook his head. 'No, I'm working.'

'Working? Oh. Who do you work for?' Erin was blunt to the point of rudeness. 'I've not seen you round here before.'

Jonah stared at the ground in embarrassment, but the stranger smiled at them and did not seem to mind. Close to, he did not look so young. His pale skin was lined around the eyes. 'No,' he said. 'You wouldn't know me. I'm not local. I'm here to...do some research in the area. I hope I didn't alarm you, appearing in the field like that.'

Jonah smiled back. 'No, of course not.'

He waited for Erin to speak, but she was still looking doubt-fully at the man. Then she asked abruptly, 'Is the fire something to do with you?'

'Well, in a way. Not that I started it,' he said easily, as Erin frowned and opened her mouth to interrupt. 'But I *am* here to try to make sure the fissure doesn't get any bigger.'

'Are you with the Forestry Commission, then?' Erin demanded.

'No,' the man replied calmly. 'I work for another company. We have interests in this part of Radnorshire. My name is Mike Golding, by the way.'

Erin's mistrust was making Jonah feel awkward. He wanted to change the subject before she said anything else. 'I'm Jonah Drake and this is Erin Morgan,' he said. 'Do you know what is causing the smoke?'

The man ran a hand through his mop of fair hair and sighed. 'I'm afraid I might do,' he said slowly.

'But what is it?' Jonah persisted. Looking at Mr Golding, he began to suspect that something was very wrong. The stranger looked strained and Jonah felt that he was far more concerned about the fire than he was willing to say.

Erin eyed the man sternly. 'Look, if you know something, you ought to tell us. My father and Jonah's uncle farm over there. If there's a forest fire, they've got to be warned.'

Mr Golding spoke gently. 'You're right. And people *will* be told, if and when it's necessary. But if I'm wrong it would be irresponsible to alarm everybody, wouldn't it? We may find that this is just a slight volcanic incident, which will soon die down.'

The children stared at each other. 'There!' cried Erin. 'I told you! Oh, this is really awful!'

'Hey, I said it might – only *might* – be a slight volcanic occurrence. Please don't go spreading alarm,' Mr Golding said. 'We don't want a lot of people trampling round in the wood to investigate.'

Erin flashed a warning look at Jonah. She didn't want him to say that he had nearly got pulled into the crack in the ground. That would really stir up trouble. He nodded very slightly to show that he understood.

Mr Golding looked at them gravely. 'You know, if you both go home and blurt this out, you could create pandemonium in the area, and all for no reason. You can see the flames aren't spreading to the trees. They are low down in the chasm. Will you keep this quiet for just a few hours? Please.'

Jonah nodded but Erin frowned.

'What do you mean by a few hours?'

'Till, say, ten o'clock tomorrow morning?'

'No! That's ages,' Erin cried. 'Tomorrow morning will be much too late. The whole forest could be alight by then!'

Mr Golding shook his head. 'No, it won't be. Honestly. If you want to meet me then – by the churchyard, say – I should know for sure what is causing it. Then you could help with the names of the farmers I might need to contact.' He held up a placatory hand, as Erin began to protest. 'This *isn't* an ordinary forest fire. The flames are deep down, like I said. There's very little danger of the trees or anything above ground catching fire.'

'But how can you be sure? And you still haven't said why – erm – a volcanic incident might be happening.' Erin was not going to be put off.

The forester looked at her steadily. 'No, and I'm not going to. Not till I know whether I am right and not till I am sure that *I* can trust *you*!'

Erin blushed scarlet. 'I'm sorry,' she mumbled. 'It's just that – well, it's not very often we see new people just walking about in this valley unless they're obviously hikers. And the smoke is, like, worrying. You know.'

'Yes, I do, so don't feel uncomfortable,' Mr Golding said, beginning to smile. He turned round suddenly. 'Oh, idiot! I've left my jacket in the porch. I'll walk back up to the church with you. If it's OK with you, that is?'

The children nodded and he fell into step beside them.

'So, are you both from farming families?'

'I am. Jonah isn't, though.'

'No, I'm just here for the summer holidays.' He smiled at Mr Golding

Erin was pacing along beside Jonah, biting her lip. 'It's strange to see fire coming up from the earth like that, isn't it?' she said, still anxious about the danger.

Mr Golding nodded. 'It *is* strange. And rather alarming.'

Jonah was reminded of the morning and suddenly felt that he could confide in this man. 'That's not the only strange thing round here,' he blurted out. 'This morning, just after it got light, I saw an animal.' Mike listened as Jonah explained what had happened. 'I thought it was going to kill me.' He stopped as they reached the wall into the churchyard. 'I was so scared!' he admitted.

'But that's terrible. A dog like that shouldn't be running

loose,' said Mr Golding. 'Look, I can't say for sure what is causing the fire, and until I *am* sure, it would be irresponsible of me to talk about my suspicions. I might well be wrong. So go home now and try not to worry. I'll see you here at ten o'clock and then I hope I will know about the fire. All right?'

They nodded, both feeling now that they could trust him.

'Good. And by the way, you can stop the Mr Golding stuff. Call me Mike. OK?'

He smiled goodbye, vaulted over the wall into the churchyard and went towards the porch to retrieve his jacket. Erin and Jonah were walking back down the lane, when they heard him shouting and turned round to see him waving at them, frantically. They exchanged puzzled glances and ran back to the church gate.

'Sorry, you two,' Mike said, 'but I feel a bit worried about you going home alone.'

Jonah was looking hard at him. 'Because of the dog?'

'Yes,' Mike answered quietly. 'It may be perfectly harmless but if a large fierce-looking dog is running loose on the hills, I think I ought to walk along with you.'

'Oh, no,' Erin exclaimed. She felt embarrassed in case Mike thought she and Jonah were too young to look after themselves. 'You don't need to do that. It's kind of you but you don't have to worry. I've got my phone. Look. And I'm used to dealing with farm dogs. We'll be careful.'

'Well, if you are sure.' Mike looked doubtful but said goodbye, raising a hand as he went through the field gate opposite. Jonah sensed that he was still uneasy about letting them go home by themselves.

'He's nice, isn't he?' he said to Erin.

'Yes, he is. Sorry about earlier.' She glanced at Jonah apologetically. 'It's just that it was so unusual to see a perfect stranger down there. I mean, we get tourists occasionally. They come to see the church. But they come up the lane by bike or car; they don't just appear in the valley. And I knew he wasn't a walker, because he wasn't wearing walking boots or anything.'

Jonah stopped in his tracks.

'What?' Erin said, turning round.

'What you just said – it made me think. Erin, where *did* he come from? And where's he going now? Like you said, there wasn't a car or a bike outside the church gate.'

'No, there wasn't! And if he's walking to wherever he is staying, why did he go across the field? There's nothing up there.' They stared at each other. 'Jonah, there's something odd about Mike. Don't you think so? He's really nice but you must admit that there's something a bit – well, a bit strange about him. Honestly, do you think he *is* a forester?'

Jonah shook his head. 'Well, to be fair, he didn't actually *say* that he's a forester. When you mentioned the Forestry Commission, he just said he worked for another company.' He grimaced. 'Perhaps we're making something out of nothing. Perhaps he *is* just a forestry manager working in the area. Anyway, we shan't know today, so we might as well go home.'

Chapter 6

DANGEROUS CREATURES

Jonah suddenly remembered that he had wanted to look at the small grey church and the old graves under the trees.

'Hey, can we go back to the churchyard?' He was fascinated by the thought of the spell on the wall inside the little church.

'Oh, yes. I forgot that's what we came for!'

Erin pushed open the gate and Jonah followed her up the path.

'It's nice,' he said, looking around at the small, round, hillocky churchyard, with its great yew tree and ancient gravestones. 'It feels friendly.'

'Dad says some people think this might have been a pagan site before Christianity arrived.'

'How do they know?'

'Because the ground is quite rounded, as if it might have been a circle once. Apparently that's a sign of a pagan holy place.' Erin grinned at him. 'And, of course, that would have been the perfect spot to build another church as "Defence Against the Dragon"!'

Jonah, bewildered, shook his head at her. 'I don't know *what* you're going on about!'

'Haven't they told you our legend?' Erin was delighted. 'Long ago, the Last Great Dragon, the Welsh dragon, went to sleep under the Radnor Forest.' Erin held her arms out and circled round. 'Right here, beneath your feet, Jonah! So the people built four churches in a ring around the forest to keep the dragon asleep and they are all dedicated to St Michael the Dragonslayer! If the link between the churches weakens, they say the dragon will wake again and ravage the countryside.'

'Wow! That would be cool,' Jonah joked, feeling even more

interested in the little church. Then a movement beyond the boundary wall flickered in the corner of his eye. 'What's that in the field?' he said. 'I just saw something move behind the bushes.' He stood still, peering at the field anxiously. 'I hope it's not that dog.'

When Erin did not answer, he turned round to find her staring up at the church roof.

'What are you looking at?' he asked.

'Sssh! Keep still,' she whispered urgently. 'There's something up there.'

Jonah peered upwards. 'I can't see anything.'

'Yes. There's some little animal on the roof.'

'Probably a cat.' Jonah wasn't particularly interested. He was still scanning the bushes for movement.

Erin suddenly clutched his arm. 'I don't believe it!' she gasped. 'It's a monkey. There, look. By the tower.'

Jonah followed her pointing finger and made out a small grey face peeking over the ridge tiles beside the tower.

'Oh, yeah. I see what you mean.'

He began to walk round to the other side of the church, to see the little creature more clearly. Erin scurried after him, and they both stood back to stare up at the roof. Clinging to the ridge tiles was a small grey animal with a head that seemed too big for its skinny body and a long, furred tail. It turned round and Erin shrieked. The creature's face was absolutely hideous. It glared down at the children with huge, bulging eyes and suddenly, with a disgusting gesture, it pulled its mouth wide with skinny fingers, leering at them. Then, screeching and gibbering, it began to prance along the roof ridge.

'That's not a monkey!'

'Whatever is it?'

Erin shuddered. 'It's horrible. I've never seen *anything* like that, before.'

'It's like – it's like a gargoyle.'

25

Erin turned to Jonah. 'Yeah, you're right! There are carvings on Hereford Cathedral that look just like that. Have you seen them?'

Jonah shook his head but kept his eyes on the grotesque little creature. 'No, I haven't been to Hereford yet. Look, there's another one! Oh, gross!'

A second ugly little animal peered round the corner of the church tower before slithering down the roof towards the children. This one was larger, with a flat, noseless face and a tail like a naked worm. It jumped up and down and began screaming at the children. The first one scrambled after it, and the creatures began to pick bits of moss and bird droppings out of the guttering to hurl at Erin and Jonah. Jonah yelled at the things and looked round for something to throw at them. He picked up a stick and hurled it at the roof. The bigger animal hissed and leapt for the drainpipe. It shinned down rapidly until it was halfway to the ground, and hung there by its bony, hairless tail, shrieking at the children.

'I don't like this!' gasped Erin in alarm, backing away. 'Come on, Jonah. Whatever they are, they're dangerous. Please let's go!'

'OK.' He was getting scared, too.

They ran for the gate, while the animals screeched in fury. They burst through and Jonah shut it firmly behind them.

'We'd better tell Bryn or your father straightaway,' he said. 'They need to catch those things before someone gets bitten. What do you think they are?'

'Dunno, but they are definitely the yuckiest little animals I've ever seen,' said Erin. 'I should think Dad will call the pest control people.'

Still feeling shaky, they walked carefully along the narrow lane between the tall hedgerows, keeping well into the side of the road and listening for vehicles. The afternoon sun warmed their faces and there was not a breath of wind, as they made their way towards Gilfach. Erin had just said again, 'But what *were* they,

Jonah?' when, suddenly, they heard an unearthly, mournful sound that lifted the hairs on the backs of their necks. They stopped walking and looked around, for a moment too frightened to move.

Erin clutched Jonah's arm. The colour drained from her face. 'What was *that*?' she whispered.

Jonah swallowed. 'It sounds – oh, no! Erin, I think it might be that dog-thing I saw this morning.' His legs seemed to tremble as he stared up at the hillside. 'I think it's up there,' he murmured, 'on the ridge.'

Erin shook with nerves as the doleful howl echoed round the valley again.

'That's not a dog, is it? It's a wolf. You know it is.'

Jonah swallowed and nodded.

Erin grabbed his hand. 'Oh, come on, quick. Let's get home.'

'Yes, but don't run! We don't want it to notice us.'

With their hearts hammering, they began to walk quickly along the lane, glancing upwards nervously. There was another howl from the animal on the hillside above them and, as they stood still in alarm, it was answered by a wailing cry from the woods on the other side of the valley.

Involuntarily, Erin screamed, and clapped her hand over her mouth. 'There's more than one!' she stammered, staring at Jonah with eyes like saucers. He began to pat his jeans pockets frantically.

'What are you doing?'

'Looking for my phone. I want to get someone to help but I think I've left it in my bedroom.'

'Oh, I've got mine.' Erin's fingers trembled as she keyed in the farm's number. Another howl rang from the woods and was answered from the hill above them again. Erin's eyes widened in fear as she put the phone to her ear. She listened for a moment and then looked at Jonah in alarm.

'I can't get a signal.' Her voice rose to a squeak. 'What are we going to do?'

Jonah tried to look calmer than he felt.

'Come on, we're nearly at your house. Hold my hand. We'll be all right.'

Chapter 7

ATTACKED

Erin's palm was clammy with fright as they hurried along the lane. Terrible howls echoed around the valley and the children's legs felt stiff and uncoordinated with fear. As they reached Gilfach farmlands, Erin pulled on Jonah's hand.

'There's a gate here,' she whispered. 'We'll be able to see across to the woods.'

They edged towards the gap in the hedge, to peer across the meadow. The fields looked peaceful and lovely, bathed in the evening sunlight. But as Jonah turned to go, the weird howl rang out again. They both jumped with shock as several huge, grey shapes sped from the woods and came racing down the sloping field straight towards them. Erin screamed and Jonah grabbed her hand.

'Run!' he yelled, pulling her along..

They sprinted along the lane, terror driving them on. Their hearts were thumping painfully. It was hard work for Erin to keep pace with Jonah's long legs but neither of them dared slow down. Soon they heard scampering sounds from the other side of the hedge and realised in panic that the wolves were gaining on them. Jonah tried to pull Erin along faster. He remembered that there was another farm gate a few yards further along the lane. He was desperate to get past, before the wolves could jump over it. Jonah felt Erin's hand tighten on his own. Her eyes were fixed on the hedge ahead of them. She had remembered the second gate, too.

With a tremendous effort, the children forced their legs to keep going. Their sides ached and they were gasping for breath. Suddenly there was a scrabbling noise and a big grey wolf leaped into the lane ahead of them. Involuntarily, the children yelled with fear. They clutched each other and backed away. Two more wolves slithered over the gate. With their great heads low to the ground and rumbling deep in their throats, they crept menacingly towards Jonah and Erin. Their muzzles were drawn back in a snarl, tongues lolling across their fangs, and their terrible eyes shone yellow.

As he backed away, Jonah put Erin behind him but suddenly she shrieked. As they both stumbled against the hedge, Jonah saw that another wolf, even larger than the others, had jumped into the lane from the hillside opposite and was standing in the road behind them. Three more wolves had come over the gate ahead. Jonah looked round wildly but there was nowhere for the children to run to. The wolves were penning them in. The children clutched each other as the animals, growling, edged nearer.

Jonah waved his arms and shouted. 'Get back! Get away!'

His voice sounded feeble and shaky, but he kept shouting. For a moment, the wolves held off but soon realised that Jonah was no threat to them. They started to move in.

The children yelled as the wolves slunk closer. Suddenly two of the brutes rushed at them. Erin leaped sideways, screaming, and the huge creatures pounced between her and Jonah. Now the other wolves moved into the gap between the children and drove Erin a few yards along the lane. The great alpha male was poised on stiffened legs, glaring at Jonah. He swallowed hard and stared back at it, trying to look defiant. He daren't move even a step towards Erin, in case he made the animals attack. Without turning his head, he risked a sideways glance. She was whimpering with terror as she backed into the thorny hedge. Her arms were bleeding and her dark curly hair was caught on the twigs. But the wolves didn't move in. They stood, motionless, in a silent ring, daring her to run.

The pack leader crouched down and looked up at Jonah

sideways. It curled back its upper lip as it fixed its eyes on him. He knew quite certainly that this was the animal he had seen that morning. *It's been stalking me!* he thought. *This is what was behind the bushes.* With its gaze still locked on Jonah, the wolf crept forward an inch or two. It stopped with a front paw raised just above the ground. Jonah could hardly breathe. Standing absolutely still, the boy and the wolf stared at each other.

Then, without warning, the monster exploded into movement, lunging at him. It crashed down on him, knocking him onto the road. Instinctively, he threw up his arms to protect his head, while the wolf, snarling horribly, closed its teeth on his shoulder, ripping at his flesh. The terrible, cracking pain made Jonah scream. It felt as if electric wires were being run through his arm. The wolf shook him violently, knocking his body up and down on the road.

The air around Jonah crackled and vibrated, and he seemed to be looking through a pane of crazed glass. Everything around him receded and he felt as if he were being sucked into a booming, whirling vortex. Out of the swirling blackness distorted faces leered, and terrible words came whispering out of the darkness. A shadowy, hooded figure bent over him. Where its face should have been, Jonah could see only blackness pierced by two glaring, reptilian eyes. Then he was stumbling through pitch-black woods with a pack of monsters hunting him down. He felt clutching hands and excruciating pain. He tried to cry out but he couldn't.

Suddenly, there were shouts and the wolf screamed against Jonah's ear. The blackness was replaced by a blinding white light, with a shimmering figure in the centre, that seemed to bend over him. Then he came round, with hard tarmac underneath him and the wolf yelping as it sprang away.

Shakily, Jonah tried to find the strength to get up. Mike Golding was some yards away along the lane thrusting a flaming branch at the animals. They snarled viciously but seemed too scared of him to attack. He swung at a wolf's eyes. It squealed and Mike rammed the branch into its side. It leapt away and ran, yowling, up the lane. Mike ran at the other wolves, brandishing the torch. They didn't wait to be struck but scrambled over the gate and fled towards the woods.

Erin struggled to untangle herself from the hedge, wincing as the thorns scratched her. Finally, pulling her tee-shirt out of the prickly branches and leaving scraps of fabric dangling, she limped over to Jonah, who lay in the lane, feeling weak and shaken. She crouched and put her arm under his shoulders, helping him to sit up.

'Oh, look at your shoulder,' she said in a wobbly voice.

Jonah's shirt was soaked in blood and ripped in shreds at the shoulder. Blood oozed out of the torn flesh around his neck. He put his right hand up to his throbbing collar-bone, trembling violently. Mike, who had stood by the gate watching until the wolves disappeared, blew the torch out and turned towards them. Now that the danger had passed, Erin couldn't stop shaking. Mike came over and gently examined Jonah's shoulder. He tore Jonah's shirt away from the wound and, taking a clean handkerchief out of his pocket, covered the bites with it.

'Hold this over it,' he said quietly to Erin and then he took off his own shirt and, with an effort, ripped off a sleeve and part of the front to make a long strip. He tied it over Jonah's shoulder and across his chest.

'This will help a bit to stop the bleeding till we can get it dressed properly.'

It felt warm and comforting. Jonah's legs started to feel less woolly.

'It's lucky that it didn't go for your face,' Mike said. 'You'll have some bad bruises, though.' He studied Jonah intently. 'How does it feel now?'

Gingerly Jonah moved his shoulder about. 'It really hurts but I suppose it could be worse.'

'Good,' said Mike. 'Let's get you home and have it attended to.'

'My house is nearest,' Erin said.

Mike stooped and helped Jonah to his feet. His legs were trembling and he clutched Erin's arm for support.

'Here. I'll carry you,' Mike said, lifting him up.

'No, it's all right, really,' Jonah protested, but his voice sounded weak. 'I can walk.'

'You're bleeding a lot. Best keep as still as you can,' said Mike firmly. 'Are you all right?' he asked, turning to Erin.

'Yes, I'm OK. Thank goodness you came!' Erin whispered.

'Yes, thanks, Mike. I don't know what—' Jonah's voice cracked and he could not go on.

Mike shook his head wearily. 'Don't thank me. That should never have happened,' he said, 'I should have trusted my instincts and insisted on walking with you. I ought to have realised the animal you saw would still be roaming around.'

Erin looked at him in misery and began to sob as she plodded along.

'Don't cry,' said Mike. 'It's all over now.'

'But it's all my fault!' she wailed. 'You said you wanted to come with us and I was all, like, we're not silly kids, thank you very much. *We* don't need help.' She kept wiping tears away with the back of her hand. 'But now look! We *did* need you. And I was so rude! I'm really sorry, Mike.'

Mike smiled at her as they turned down the lane towards Gilfach Farm. 'You weren't rude. A bit blunt, maybe.'

Erin was shaking her head. 'You're kind but—'

'Erin, it wasn't at all silly to be cautious. I'm a stranger here. You don't know the first thing about me. Now stop upsetting yourself. I mean it,' he said, as she looked up and shook her head miserably. 'It wasn't your fault at all. Come on, cheer up.'

Jonah was thinking Mike must be pretty fit to carry him so far without getting out of breath. He hadn't seemed to be afraid of the wolves, either. That reminded him.

'What about the farmers?' he blurted out. 'They need to know what's happening. People will have heard the wolves and they'll be scared stiff.'

'Yes,' put in Erin. 'I expect Dad and Bryn and the others are already out with their guns.'

'Do you think they've escaped from a zoo?' Jonah asked, looking into Mike's grim face, as he strode along.

Erin shook her head, sniffing back her tears. 'But how could that happen? I can understand one of them getting out but not a pack of them. It doesn't make sense.'

'We're nearly at your house, Erin. I need to talk to your parents and everyone else in the area,' said Mike. 'Something has to be done. We have to alert the community round here, or there's going to be a terrible accident.'

Chapter 8

CRISIS

As they hurried up the drive and into the farmyard at Gilfach, the kitchen door was thrown open and Gwen Morgan looked out.

'Oh, my goodness, what's happened?' she cried, staring at Erin, and Mike with Jonah in his arms. Her eyes widened as she noticed Mike had no shirt under his blood-stained jacket, and that there was blood oozing from Jonah's bandages and from the great scratches on Erin's arms. Erin flew to her.

'It was wolves, Mam! They went for Jonah and me.' Erin extricated herself from her mother's arms. 'This is Mike. He saved our lives. He saved us from the wolves.' She began to cry again with shock and Jonah, near to tears himself, began to tell her mother what had happened.

Quietly, Mike intervened. 'Have you some ointment and bandages, Mrs Morgan?'

'*Wolves?* I can't take this in. I heard an awful noise but wolves—are you sure?' Mrs Morgan looked bewildered for a moment, but her practical streak quickly took over, and she turned to Jonah. 'Well then, *cariad*, let's get you into the house, so that I can see to your shoulder.' She led the way into the kitchen and took a large first-aid kit out of a cupboard, while Erin ran upstairs to her bedroom to find a clean tee-shirt for herself and one that would fit Jonah.

'And get a shirt of your father's for Mike, while you're up there,' her mother called after her. As she washed and dressed Jonah's wound, Mike explained what had happened in the lane.

'The noise you heard really *was* wolves howling, Gwen,' Jonah put in, shakily. 'They came out of the woods and one, a huge one, came over the hill. You know, the one that chased me this morning. It wasn't a dog.' It was difficult to talk. There seemed to be a lump in his throat that he couldn't swallow. 'They would have killed us, if it hadn't been for Mike.'

Mrs Morgan was staring at Mike in horror.

'But how can they be wolves? Have they escaped from a zoo or somewhere? Where have they come from?' she said, pausing as she secured dressing strips to Jonah's wound.

Mike looked at her gravely. 'I'm sorry but I don't think I should take time to talk now. I need to get on and alert other people quickly.'

Mrs Morgan shut the first-aid box and stood up, putting her arms tightly round Jonah and Erin, who had come downstairs with an old blue tee-shirt for him and a check shirt for Mike. She looked at him. 'I don't know how to thank you.' Her eyes were watery.

Erin stroked her mother's hand. 'It's all right, Mam. We're safe.'

Slowly, Mrs Morgan released the children, sniffed back her tears and smiled at Mike. 'I'm sorry. Oh, dear, I'm being a bit over-emotional.' She wiped her hand over her eyes and turned briskly to Jonah. 'Well, now, we must get you to A and E.'

Jonah groaned. 'Do I have to, Gwen? Now you've dressed it, I'm sure it will be OK. I don't think the hospital could do much more, could they?'

'Well, maybe not,' she said, 'but I think Claire or I should run you into Presteigne, at least, and let our doctor look at it. You might need stitches. I'll go and phone her now.'

In a moment or two, she came back into the kitchen, looking annoyed. 'Would you believe it?' she said. 'I can't get a signal. It was all right at lunchtime. Oh, well, I'll have to use my mobile.' She took her smartphone out of a dresser drawer, dialled and put the phone to her ear. She frowned, checked the code and pressed the connect button again. Then she put the phone down. 'Do you know,' she said to Mike, 'that is very odd. This one isn't working either.'

'Neither is mine,' Erin put in. 'I tried to phone when we heard the wolves.'

Mike looked at her thoughtfully. 'Do you mind?' he said to Mrs Morgan, going over to the light switch beside the kitchen door. He flicked the switch and the light came on.

'Well, you have electricity,' he said. 'There must be something wrong with the telephone network.' Jonah noticed that Mike was chewing his lip for a moment, deep in thought.

'Oh, that's so annoying!' exclaimed Mrs Morgan. 'Just when we need to phone. Well, I'd better drive you to the Community Hospital at Kington then, Jonah. We can call in at Bryn's on the way.'

Mike stood looking down for a moment. Then he straightened up, as if he had come to a decision.

'I don't think you should leave the farm just now, Mrs Morgan. I'm not sure it would be safe.'

Gwen Morgan stared at him. Then her face cleared. 'Oh, in case these dogs…'

'Mam!'

'All right, Erin. Sorry. In case these *wolves* attack the cattle?'

Mike looked uncomfortable. 'I think there might be a serious situation developing, that needs to be tackled quickly,' he said. 'It would be best if we could get everyone who lives in the area together. Then we can tell everybody what's happened and talk about what we should do. I ought to go.'

'I see,' Gwen Morgan said slowly and then nodded. 'But before you start, I think you all need a cup of tea,' she said. 'A good hot drink will make Jonah and Erin feel better. You, too,' she added to Mike, 'before you rush off. You need something to keep you going. Erin, there's some *bara brith* in the larder that I made this morning. Bring the butter too, *cariad*.'

Just as they settled down with mugs of tea and slices of fruit bread thickly spread with butter, they heard vehicles in the farmyard and Mr Morgan came in with his farmhand, Ted, followed by Bryn and his brother, Rhodri.

'Do you know that none of the phone landlines are working, Gwen, and we can't use our mobiles either!' announced Emlyn Morgan. 'I've driven all up the valley and I've been right round by Pilleth as far as Bleddfa. Nothing's working! Bryn was on his way here to see if we knew what was happening. A couple of us will have to go into town to see what we can do.'

'We can't get a signal anywhere,' put in Ted.

Emlyn went across to the radio, and noticed Mike. 'Oh, hello there,' he said, nodding to him, as he switched it on. There was a buzz of talking, as Rhodri greeted Jonah, whom he had not seen since Bryn's wedding, and Mrs Morgan introduced Mike to everyone.

'Oh, I've forgotten your surname,' she exclaimed.

Mike smiled. 'Don't worry, Mrs Morgan. Just "Mike" will do.'

Emlyn was switching from channel to channel on the radio. 'Nothing,' he exclaimed. 'I can't get a signal.' He looked at the electric kettle, which Mrs Morgan had filled again. 'Well, the kettle's boiling. So it's not the whole electricity supply. That's a bit odd.'

'And did you hear some terrible howling noises?' put in Bryn. 'A few minutes ago? Like a pack of dogs or something?'

Gwen Morgan stood up. 'I'll get some more *bara brith*,' she began to say, but then her voice faltered and she had to turn away.

'Gwen!' Emlyn Morgan stared at his wife in consternation. 'What ever is the matter, love?'

'I've something to tell you,' she said in a wobbly voice. 'That howling, Bryn. Erin and Jonah were nearly killed this afternoon. We have Mike to thank for saving them.'

The new arrivals stared.

'What happened?' asked Rhodri. Then he noticed the plasters

showing at the neck of Jonah's tee-shirt. 'What's the matter with your shoulder?'

Quietly, Mike answered for him. 'Jonah was bitten but don't worry. It's just a flesh wound and bad bruising, thankfully.' He stopped and looked round the table, as if wondering how best to explain. 'Just now, as they were coming home from the church, the children were attacked by...' He paused and looked uncomfortably at the wondering faces. 'By some wolves,' he finished.

The adults gaped at him.

Bryn turned to Jonah. 'Wolves! That's impossible! There are no wolves in Wales!' Distractedly he ran his hand through his black hair. 'I can't believe you said that.'

Emlyn Morgan leaned against the fridge with his arms folded, eyes narrowed cynically, as he surveyed Mike Golding. 'By here,' he said slowly, 'we don't believe in fairy stories. The last wolf in Wales was shot more than a hundred years ago, just up the road in Bleddfa.' He straightened up and locked eyes with the young man. 'I don't appreciate you filling these kids' heads with nonsense, see? Bad enough that they were set on by a pack of dogs, without you making them too scared to leave the house.'

'Mr Morgan, I...' Mike started to say but Erin butted in.

'They *were* wolves, Dad. They were!'

Emlyn ruffled her dark brown curls.

'I know you thought they were, *cariad*, but let's just be rational, eh? It would have been on the news, stands to reason, if a whole pack of wolves had escaped from somewhere.'

Erin twisted away, her face reddening and angry tears filling her eyes.

'Dad, you weren't there. We're not silly kids. They were *wolves*! Take a look at Jonah's bite, why don't you? And, anyway, the radio's not working, so you couldn't have heard about it!' She slammed out of the kitchen and they could hear her furious sobs, as she thumped up the stairs. Mrs Morgan shook her head at her husband.

'Oh, Emlyn! Did you have to? You can see how upset she is.' She turned apologetically to Mike. 'It's just that it is so difficult to believe that there could be wolves on the loose in Wales.'

Emlyn sniffed but said no more. There was an awkward pause and then Bryn said quietly, 'Are you sure it wasn't a pack of dogs, Jonah?'

Jonah nodded vigorously. 'Yes, they definitely weren't German Shepherds or anything, and they were much too big to be huskies. I've seen one of them before! It was the thing that chased me this morning. But I knew nobody would believe me if I said it was a wolf.' He shivered as he remembered the animal's evil yellow eyes.

'But a wolf bite!' Rhodri Morgan said. 'Surely, if the animal had been a wolf, Jonah would have far worse injuries. A wolf's jaws are much more powerful than a dog's. If it had been a wolf, it could well have bitten through the boy's shoulder-bone!'

Mike nodded. 'You're right. But, you see, it didn't get a chance to shake Jonah about too much. Before it could close its teeth fast and really bite down, I shoved a burning branch in its face.'

Rhodri nodded but Jonah thought he still seemed rather sceptical. 'Lucky you had time to find something big enough to light,' he said.

Mike looked around at the doubting faces. 'I heard the wolves well before they attacked,' he said calmly.

'Look, they were *wolves*,' Jonah insisted. He was beginning to feel annoyed now. 'We had quite enough time to look at them. And we saw other things, too.' He laughed hollowly. 'Now this will really make you think Erin and I are off our rockers.'

Chapter 9

AN UNBELIEVABLE STORY

Jonah told them everything. He described how they had found the great, smoking fissure in the ground and how he had felt himself slipping towards the crevice. Turning to see how Mike would react, he told them about the strange, disgusting little animals on top of the church. Mike's lips tightened as Jonah described what he and Erin had seen, but he said nothing. Suddenly, Jonah broke off as a thought occurred to him.

'What is it?' asked Claire.

'When my foot got caught,' he said slowly, 'Erin swore she saw a bony hand round my ankle. And I didn't feel as if I was just slipping, either,' he added. 'It felt as if something was pulling me! It could have been one of those awful things on the church. *They* had nasty skinny hands. It could have been one of them!'

When he finished talking there was silence for a moment. The adults seemed lost for words. Then, abruptly, Emlyn turned to Mike. 'I have to see for myself. I can't take it on board, otherwise. If you can show me just one of the things Jonah has been talking about, I'll be able to believe everything else.' He turned to the other men. 'I need to go up to the church. Do you want to come?'

Mike placed his hands on the table. 'I told your wife that I have to call a meeting to alert as many people as possible. Look, we need to take action fast, if we are to prevent a disaster. People could get hurt. If we go to the church now, quickly, and if I can convince you that we have a serious problem here, will you help me get word around the community?'

The men nodded. 'Come on, then,' said Emlyn. 'I'll get my guns.'

As Emlyn spoke, Jonah noticed a strange expression flicker

across Mike's face. Then he nodded.

'Right,' he said.

Emlyn came back into the room with a couple of shotguns. 'Right, then, lads. Are you going back to Maesglas to fetch guns for yourself and Rhodri?' he asked Bryn.

'Yes, and I'll bring Claire here, if it's OK. I don't like the idea of her being at the farm alone, if there are really wolves around.'

Bryn left the farmhouse and was soon back with Claire, and two shotguns.

Emlyn turned to Gwen. 'Now you lock yourselves in. Don't go outside until we're back. We won't be long.'

'I don't like this,' said Gwen. 'You're putting yourselves in danger, for no good reason. Why can't you just take Mike's word?'

Rhodri patted her shoulder. 'It's OK, Gwen, really. Even if we did meet wolves, they'd be unlikely to attack five grown men. Especially when they hear the guns. Don't you worry.'

The men went out into the farmyard. At the kitchen door, Emlyn turned round. 'Tell Erin where I've gone,' he said to Gwen. 'And tell her I'm sorry. I could have handled that better.' He shut the door behind him, and Gwen and Claire looked at each other nervously.

'I don't know about you,' Gwen said, 'but I could do with another cuppa. While I make it, would you go up and tell Erin to come down now? I'd be happier if we were all in the same room, until the men get back.'

Gwen made more tea and the four of them gathered round the kitchen table. They all sat rigidly, straining to listen for any noise outside. Erin's eyes were still red from crying but she managed a watery smile, when her mother hugged her.

'They'll soon be back, Mam,' she began, 'and then—'

She was cut off by a terrible howl from the direction of the church. Her hand flew to her mouth. They all jumped to their feet and then they heard a commotion of shouts and snarling. Claire turned to Gwen.

'Get me a shotgun, Gwen,' she said. 'I'm going outside. Don't worry,' she added, as the other woman faltered. 'I'm a good shot.'

But before Gwen had time to fetch one from the gun-rack in the study, the men came running back down the farm drive and spilled into the kitchen.

'Erin, I owe you an apology, my love,' said her father sombrely. 'And Mike and Jonah. You were right all along.'

Just as the men were coming back from the church, where they had a glimpse of the nasty little creatures the children had seen on the roof, the wolves had come down from the woods. They had sprung into the lane again, but the five men had been able to hold them off for long enough to sprint back to the farmhouse.

'But it was weird. None of us got a decent shot at them,' Rhodri said.

Ted turned to Emlyn. 'Don't you think we ought to get your animals inside, Boss?'

'Good point. We must round them up right away,' said Emlyn.

'Yes, let's get the stock in the barns first, and then we have to get out and warn local people quickly,' Bryn said urgently, 'or someone's going to be killed.'

Emlyn suddenly stared at Bryn, and then looked round the group. '*Someone's going to get killed*,' he repeated softly. 'Yet have you noticed? We've six or seven ferocious predators in the valley but not a single sheep nor any of your cattle, Bryn, seem to have been hurt.' He looked round the group. 'They aren't hunting to eat.'

It was true. Bryn's Hereford cattle and all the sheep in the meadows along the lane seemed perfectly calm and undisturbed.

'It's people they are after,' said Bryn, slowly.

'Somehow,' said Gwen, 'that makes the situation more frightening. We have to let everyone know.'

'Well, we can't phone. I suggest we go now and bring in the livestock, and then we can drive around,' said Bryn.

'If we leave word at one house among, say, six or seven, they can pass the message along to the others. That way, we could reach most people,' Ted offered.

'Good thinking. Where should everyone meet?'

Rhodri, who had been sitting silently, listening, now spoke. 'How wide an area do you need to cover? You aren't talking just about this valley, are you?'

Mike shook his head. 'We need to reach anyone who lives near enough to come to Cascob church tomorrow morning.'

The adults, who were already very worried, now looked completely mystified.

'Why at the church?' Claire wanted to know. 'Outside the pub in Bleddfa, on the green there, would be better, surely? I know the landlord would—'

Rhodri cut in. 'Sorry, Claire, but we don't have time now. Let's do as Mike asks, till he has time to explain.' He stood up. 'Mike, if we want to use the churchyard, I think we should go to Knighton and see the vicar. Why don't I take you on my motorbike? Afterwards we can get around people in Bleddfa.' He turned to the others. 'If we all take different villages, and call on a couple of houses in each street, we shall soon get people to pass the word to their neighbours. All right?'

Erin sprang to her feet. 'Jonah and I can do New Radnor. Jonah could borrow Dad's bike, couldn't he? Or we can go on the ponies,' she said, and Jonah nodded eagerly.

Ted grinned at them. 'On ponies? The wolves would think lunch was coming!'

'And with Jonah's bad shoulder and both of you in shock!' Gwen exclaimed. 'You're going nowhere. You are staying here.'

'No way!' said Emlyn firmly. 'Not alone here with wolves on the loose, Gwen. Let them go with one of the adults in a car.'

'I'll see to Cascob,' offered Ted. When the sheep and cattle were in, Bryn and Claire would drive to the villages along the road running north of the Radnor forest, and Emlyn and Gwen would take the southern route.

'Get as many people as you can,' Mike said, 'to the churchyard by half-past seven tomorrow morning.'

Ted began to object. 'You'll never get people to the church at that time.'

Mike leaned forward. 'The earlier the better. We can't leave things as they are for long. It's urgent. We have to get round as many houses as possible tonight and ask people to come to a meeting tomorrow. We have to take action straightaway! Just tell them there will be information about the telephone blackouts, and – er – some worrying happenings in this area. That's probably all you will need to say, for the moment.'

As they all went out, Jonah noticed Bryn take Rhodri aside and heard him ask quietly, 'Do you think Mike genuinely has some special information?'

Rhodri nodded. 'Yes, I do.'

'Are we talking about terrorism here?'

Jonah stared. He couldn't believe what Bryn had just asked. Terrorists? Here in Radnorshire? And using *wolves*? He looked across at Rhodri.

'I don't want to speculate about who Mike is, or where his information is coming from but my instincts tell me he can be trusted,' Rhodri said to Bryn, adding grimly, 'I just hope I am right!'

Chapter 10

WHO IS MIKE?

By a quarter past seven the next morning, a crowd of anxious villagers were milling about in the little churchyard. Bryn had worried that parked cars would cause chaos in the narrow, hilly lane, so he was pleased to see that Rhodri and Ted had parking well under control, directing cars into one of Emlyn's fields a hundred yards or so from the church.

Jonah saw Erin arrive with her parents and slipped across to join her. They smiled at each other, both aware of the tense atmosphere. He noticed that people were glancing around anxiously and chattering in low voices. They all seemed to be discussing why their phones and televisions wouldn't work. Everyone realised that if the vicar and the parish councillors wanted a meeting this early in the morning, something must be seriously wrong. Some people in the crowd looked very worried, particularly mothers holding small children.

'Where is Mike?' Bryn asked, frowning. 'No point bringing everyone here without him. Go and see if you can find him, kids.'

Jonah and Erin walked out of the lych-gate to watch the people coming up the lane.

'How's your shoulder?' Erin asked.

He waggled it experimentally. 'Do you know?' he said. 'It's only just a bit sore. The pain was *terrible* when the wolf was biting me. I was like, it's going to kill me. I'd have thought I wouldn't be able to move it for weeks, but it hardly hurts at all, now. Don't you think that's a bit weird?' He remembered the terrifying faces swirling round him in the blackness as the wolf's jaws had closed on him. Thinking about it made him feel shivery and so uncomfortable that he couldn't bring himself to talk about that part yet.

Erin was looking thoughtful. 'Yes, it is weird. Look, Jonah, when you were lying on the ground, blood was pouring out and there was this great flap of flesh, sort of hanging down. Stomach-turning! The wolf almost ripped your shoulder off. I thought you would have to have an operation. But it's as if you just got scratched a bit.' She hesitated, looking down at her feet. 'You know, when Mike bandaged your bite? He looked – well – sort of far away and intent. Oh, I can't explain. It's just that there's something about him, something – I don't know – it's as if he's someone quite different from who he says he is. I don't mean he's sinister,' she added hastily, as Jonah started to object. 'I just mean that I'm sure there's more to Mike than he's telling us.'

Jonah nodded slowly. 'Yeah, you could be right.'

'You don't think,' Erin said thoughtfully, 'that he's SAS, do you?'

'What, in the Army, you mean?'

'Well, of course, fluff-brain. Special Air Services.'

Jonah stared. 'How come?'

'Well,' she continued, 'they're trained to do special combat and they go behind enemy lines, don't they? And they work in secret to search for terrorists and everything. Look how Mike fought off the wolves all by himself. He obviously knows about combat. Yeah? And when I asked if he worked for the Forestry Commission—'

'He said he worked for *another company*!' Jonah broke in. 'You could be right! They talk about "companies" in the Army, don't they?' He thought for a moment and moved closer to speak quietly into Erin's ear. 'I heard Rhodri talking to Bryn last night. He said he felt he could trust Mike. *And* he wondered if Mike was here to investigate terrorism.'

Erin's eyes widened. 'Well, that sounds like the SAS to me. And Rhodri would know.'

Jonah wrinkled his forehead. 'Why?'

Erin stared. 'Don't you know? Didn't anyone tell you?'

'No. Tell me what?'

Erin shook her head, big-eyed. 'I can't believe you've been related to him for six months and you still don't know.'

Jonah made a mock grinding sound with his teeth. 'I may have to injure you. *What* don't I know?'

Erin was delighted. 'He was in the *Regiment*.'

Jonah looked puzzled. 'What regiment?'

'No, not any old regiment. *The* Regiment! You know, near Hereford?' Erin made googly eyes. 'Oh, crikey, Mastermind, do you need to ring a friend?'

'Hey! Cut it out.' Jonah said, laughing. 'I don't know what you're on about. And you don't ring a friend on 'Mastermind', anyway.'

Erin threw a weary glance upwards. 'There's a pretty famous Army HQ near Hereford. No? Doesn't ring a bell? Rhodri was stationed there, Jonah. He was in the *SAS*!'

'Rhodri was in the SAS? Really? Wowzers!'

'The penny drops!'

Jonah grinned. 'Nobody said! I just knew he'd been in the Army. I didn't even know the SAS were based near here.'

'Well, they are, and I wouldn't mind betting Mike's one of them. He's so calm and sort of quietly in control. He's just the type.'

Jonah nodded thoughtfully. People were still going through the lych-gate and Erin waved to several children who went to her school.

'I thought you said there weren't any other kids our age in the valley,' Jonah said.

'There aren't. They all live round the Radnor Forest, though. I'll introduce you after the meeting,' she told Jonah. 'You'll like Gethin. That tall boy just going up the path. He's great at rugby.'

The children kept scanning the crowd for Mike. Jonah looked at a trickle of people filing through the gate. The little church was coming alive today, with so many people here.

Standing on tiptoe to get a better view, Erin commented. 'If we had this many people here every Sunday, the church wouldn't weaken.'

A small shadowy thought stirred in Jonah's mind.

'Erin,' he said urgently. 'What exactly did you say about the churches round the Forest?'

'That if the link weakened,' Erin said patiently, 'the dragon would come out.'

Jonah clutched her sleeve and drew her to one side. 'Erin,' he said in a low voice, 'the link *is* weakening, isn't it? This church is hardly used. What if the smoke means—'

'—that the dragon *is* waking up,' Erin finished, her eyes wide.

Jonah's mouth was dry and he felt shivery with excitement. 'It could be the dragon, couldn't it? What if the old legends were true, Erin? What if it comes up here?'

They stared at each other. Then Erin frowned and bit her lip in thought. 'Those horrible monkey-things we saw,' she began slowly. 'If the hand that grabbed you did belong to one of those things...'

'It was going to pull me down to the dragon.'

'To feed it? You could have been its dinner!'

Jonah shivered. 'Thanks for that!' Then another thought struck him. 'Hey, you said the monkey-things reminded you of gargoyles on the cathedral. And the gargoyles were supposed to remind people of all the horrible things waiting in Hell, weren't they? What if they've come up through that chasm in the ground?'

'Like the dragon's cracked the ground and let them out?'

'Yes, and you know what?' Jonah said excitedly. 'I bet that's why Mike's here. I bet the SAS or MI5 or something found out about it.'

Erin screwed up her face. 'But how?'

'Well, I dunno. But you said yourself that there was something kind of special about him.'

They were so preoccupied that they did not notice Bryn beckoning to them. Jonah stared unseeingly at his feet, while he thought about all the implications. Erin looked up and saw Bryn striding towards them.

She shook Jonah's arm. 'Bryn's coming,' she said urgently. 'Act normal and don't say anything. No one will believe us yet.'

Bryn waved from the churchyard wall. 'Mike's here.'

Jonah nodded meaningfully at Erin. 'See what I mean?' he said. 'How come he got in without us seeing him?'

Erin shook the thoughts away and began to grin. 'Over the wall from the field, I expect, Dr Watson!' Then she ran back through the gate, as Jonah groaned.

Chapter 11

THE MEETING

It was half past seven. Emlyn Morgan beckoned Erin and Jonah to come over, and introduced them to a tall, balding man with a kind face, who was talking quietly with some other clergymen.

'This is my daughter, Mr Vaughan,' Emlyn said, putting a hand on Erin's shoulder, 'and this is Claire and Bryn Parry's nephew, Jonah Drake. Jonah's the one who got bitten by the wolf yesterday. This is the Vicar of Knighton, you two.'

He introduced Jonah and Erin to the other ministers, who shook their heads, appalled by the thought of a wolf attack.

'Exactly what happened, Jonah?' The vicar looked at him keenly, as Mike came up to the group.

'I think we should start the meeting, if you don't mind,' he said quietly. 'It's after half past seven now and everyone else will want to hear what happened to the children.'

'Of course.' The vicar walked forward with Mike until they were at the highest point of the churchyard. Then he raised his arms to get everyone's attention.

Someone called out, 'I think we're ready to start, everybody.'

The crowd moved forward expectantly. Fingers of early sunlight crept across the churchyard, giving an unreal atmosphere to the almost silent gathering. Jonah felt as if he might be dreaming. The beautiful little building, with its quaint bell tower, looked so timeless and peaceful in the early light, that it was hard to believe in the weird things he and Erin had just been talking about.

'I want to thank you all for spreading the news of this meeting,' said the vicar. 'I'm impressed that so many of you have managed to come here at this time of the morning.' He looked gravely around the throng of people. 'I am James Vaughan, the Vicar of Knighton, and this gentleman is Mike Golding. By now, you have all realised that since yesterday we have been cut off from the world outside. There have been no phones working in this area, no radio and no television. I know how very difficult this is in a farming community. But the main reason for asking you to come here is because most of you have heard about the worrying incidents in this valley yesterday. I'll hand over now to Mike, who can tell us more.'

The crowd muttered and stirred, but quickly settled to listen again, all their eyes glued to Mike's face.

'Good morning, everyone. Thank you very much for making the effort to come. I know you all need to get to work but I wanted as many people as possible to find out what is going on here. I have been sent to Wales to assess what could become a serious situation. Something is happening which you will find very hard to believe.' He grinned ruefully. 'In fact, when you have heard what I have to say, you may well think I'm mad, but I promise you I am not.'

People exchanged puzzled glances.

Erin nudged Jonah. 'Bet they won't believe there are wolves about,' she muttered.

'Those of you who live anywhere near here may have heard a terrible howling noise in the valley yesterday afternoon.' There was a buzz of talking and several people nodded. Mike beckoned to Jonah, who went to stand self-consciously beside him. 'Lots of you know Bryn Parry from Maesglas Farm. Well, this is his wife's nephew. Yesterday Jonah was with Erin Morgan from Gilfach Farm, just down the lane here, when he was bitten by one of the animals you heard.' He looked around for a moment at the tense faces and then said quietly: 'The children were attacked by a pack of wolves.'

There was an immediate hubbub and cries of 'Rubbish' and 'Come off it!'

Jonah looked towards Erin, who rolled her eyes.

Mike raised a hand for silence. 'I know, I know. But I was there when Jonah was bitten. I was lucky to be able to drive them off. And, no, they weren't German Shepherd dogs, as I can hear some people suggesting. They were very large, *grey wolves*.'

An old, ruddy-faced man in a tweed cap, who looked as if he might be a farmer, scoffed. 'You're dreaming, boyo. Hasn't anyone told you wolves are extinct in Britain?'

Someone yelled, 'They want to bring them back to Scotland though!'

'Maybe they are starting here,' called a young, laughing man near the front. 'My village isn't called Bleddfa for nothing!'

People started to laugh. Jonah looked around, perplexed. 'He means that Bleddfa is Welsh for *Place of the Wolf*,' said one of the clergymen, smiling.

Emlyn Morgan pushed forward and raised his voice so that everyone could hear him. 'The animals *were* wolves,' he declared. 'It wasn't just the children who saw them. Bryn and Rhodri Parry here, and Ted Lewis, were with Mr Golding and me when the wolves came out of the woods behind my farm. We saw them close up and there was no doubting what they were.'

Above the clamour a woman shouted, 'Where did they come from, then?'

'That's one of the things I am here to find out,' Mike replied calmly, 'but another strange thing happened that you should know about.

'Erin Morgan and Jonah Drake met me yesterday, after they had been looking at a huge fissure in the field over there,' Mike pointed, 'where smoke is puffing out. You must have noticed it. Look, there it goes again, now!'

People craned their necks to follow the line of Mike's outstretched arm. There was a swell of conversation as the crowd watched a large column of smoke rise into the air and hang above the woodland.

The young man standing in front of Mike raised his hand. 'I felt concerned,' he called out, 'so I went into the woods to look. The smoke's coming from deep under the ground!'

'Smoke where no smoke should be,' Mike said clearly. 'And then, a bit later on, Jonah and Erin saw two creatures, looking just like gargoyles, scuttling all over the church.'

There was a roar of laughter. 'Like *gargoyles*?'

'Over-active imaginations at work there!'

'Kids saw some animals and got scared, innit?' someone called. 'Sure t' be.'

Jonah heard the word 'squirrels' and frowned. He went back to stand with Erin.

'They think we're just stupid little kids,' he muttered.

She tossed her curls back. 'Don't worry about it. We know what we saw.'

The farmer in the tweed cap, who was standing on the edge of the crowd, grinned round mirthlessly. 'Seeing as the phone lines are dead, I'd like to know how you knew about this smoking chasm in the wood before you got here,' he said, confrontationally. 'Have you got a different kind of mobile phone from the rest of us?'

Mike met his gaze evenly. 'The information came by courier. What I think we should—' He was interrupted by a mournful wail that sounded in the fields beyond the church.

Everyone started in alarm. 'What was that?'

Then there were answering cries from the hills – strange, doleful howls that raised hairs on the backs of people's necks.

'Wolves! There really *are* wolves.' The whisper ran through the crowd. Nobody looked sceptical now. Everyone stared up at the hills, while the howls echoed eerily round the valley.

A woman cuddling two small children cried out in a frightened voice, 'What can we do?'

Mike raised his hands for quiet. 'I asked for this meeting because we need to have a plan to ensure your safety, when you have to leave your homes,' he said. 'These animals are extremely aggressive and the danger is worse while you have no telephones. For the time being, you shouldn't go out alone.'

The mood among the villagers changed. People looked at Mike, standing quietly in front of them, and now felt they could trust him. The crowd drew closer together, their eyes fixed on the wooded ridge above the church. A light breeze was wafting the pungent smoke across the churchyard. There was an outbreak of coughing. To the alarm of the villagers, sparks and tiny tongues of flame rose in the column of smoke from among the trees.

The Reverend Vaughan stepped forward. In his clear voice he said, 'Let us pray for strength to help us deal with this strange situation, and for the safety of everyone in this community.' The crowd stood motionless, heads bent and hands holding hands tightly, as the vicar started to pray. Then a child's high voice rose above the prayers.

'Mummy, look at the monkey!'

People nearby turned to look at the little boy.

'Sssh, Jacky,' muttered his mother anxiously. 'It's just a pussy-cat.'

'No, it isn't,' the child shouted. 'Look. Up on the roof. It's a monkey.'

Erin and Jonah gasped.

'Oh no!' Erin said and then she stepped forward, evading Emlyn's restraining hand, and called out. 'It's one of the animals we saw yesterday.'

Everyone who could hear her faltered in their prayers and stared up at the roof. Something skittered across the slates, whisking its tail. Girls screamed and the crowd broke up, as people backed away from the church. Several hideous little creatures suddenly appeared on the roof ridge, screaming abuse and threatening the flabbergasted faces turned up to them. An elderly man turned and rushed towards the lych-gate. And then, from the woodland deep in the Radnor Forest, came a great rumbling noise. The earth seemed to pulse and shiver beneath their feet and, high above the trees, a great column of fire shot into the sky.

Chapter 12

LEGENDS OF RADNOR FOREST

Some people began to scream as the plume of smoke mushroomed above the woodland beyond the stream. Neighbours clung to each other and looked apprehensively from the woods to the church roof, though the grotesque little animals seemed to have vanished.

The man in the tweed cap strode towards Mike and said aggressively, 'I want to be told what you know about this smoke. We need that information now. And no flannel, boyo. Give it us straight.' He looked at Mr Vaughan apologetically. 'Sorry, Vicar. I don't mean any harm but we need to understand what we're dealing with.'

Mike smiled at him. 'Don't worry. I understand how you feel.' He raised his voice. 'This is what we believe is happening. Please bear with me because it's going to sound very strange. I am glad that your local ministers are able to be here today because it all has to do with the local churches and, in particular, this church.' He stopped for a second and glanced round at the old building bathed in the early morning sunlight. Then he turned to the sea of faces in front of him.

'Look,' he said, 'around the Radnor Forest there are four churches all dedicated to Saint Michael – this one, and those at Cefnllys, Llanfihangel Rhydithon and Llanfihangel Nantmelon. And you all know that in English *Llanfihangel* means the sacred place of the angel.'

All their eyes were fixed on Mike as he reminded them how the old legend told that after the Archangel Michael's victory over the Red Dragon of Wales, *Y Ddraig Goch*, those churches were built to keep it asleep under the Forest. The legend prophesied that the dragon would wake up if the ancient link between the four Forest churches of St Michael the Dragonslayer should ever be broken.

'There are only a few houses out here at Cascob, so it isn't worth opening the church every Sunday,' he said. 'There's only one service a month. One might say it hardly counts as a centre of worship any more.'

'So are you saying that here, at Cascob, the link is almost severed?' asked one of the other clergymen.

Mike nodded. 'The thing is, it's not just an old legend. The last Great Dragon has been here, under Radnor Forest, all the time, and I'm afraid that the smoke we can see shows that it is actually waking up.'

A howl of protest rose from the crowd. There were some catcalls and jeering.

'That can't be true. We're in the twenty-first century, for heaven's sake,' someone shouted. 'That's just stories, sure t' be.'

'It's probably a bit of volcanic action,' someone else called out.

People started to chatter amongst themselves. Some, grinning cynically, were asking how this young chap could expect anyone to take him seriously. Others pointed at the church roof, where they had all seen the horrible little animals, as proof that something weird was happening. Mike held up his arms to quieten everyone and the villagers turned back to look up at him. His quiet dignity, as he waited for everyone's attention, stopped many of them from leaving. There was a lot of head-shaking, until another ominous rumble from the woods made everyone turn to stare anxiously at the column of smoke.

'I'm sorry but it really isn't just a legend,' Mike said. 'I know it sounds incredibly silly, but I am in earnest when I tell you that the dragon *is* waking up!' He looked gravely around the crowd of people. He seemed suddenly to be taller and straighter, and his blond hair glowed in the sun. Jonah stared at him. What was it about Mike? Something pricked at the back of his mind.

He turned to Erin. 'I keep getting this weird feeling I've seen Mike before. Can't think where, though.'

She stared at Mike through narrowed eyes. 'That's funny, because I'm getting that feeling, too. Do you think he might have been on TV?'

'Yeah, you could be right,' Jonah said. 'Maybe he's been interviewed or something.'

Mike was telling the crowd that the creatures on the roof weren't animals. 'They are small demons.'

There was an appalled buzz of conversation.

Mike raised his voice. 'In the West, dragons have always been associated in people's minds with terror, and I think that these Night Creatures, as we call them, are seizing an opportunity.'

He turned towards The Reverend Vaughan, who nodded in agreement.

'As you well know,' said the vicar, 'people long ago didn't have to see demons to be sure they existed. You even have an *Abracadabra* spell on the church wall here. But in the modern world very few of us believe in anything like that. We put bad things down to accidents, disease, human nastiness and so on.'

'And that means,' said Mike, 'that it is much harder nowadays for the Night Creatures to spread fear. I think the Underworld is hoping to benefit from the chaos and terror the dragon will almost certainly cause when it wakes.'

'So these creatures think the dragon will attack us?' the vicar said.

'Yes, and they will use anything they can to frighten you. They might try to enter human or animal bodies, or they might use stone effigies – like gargoyles. The more people who see them, the more the terror will spread. Your fear will help their power to grow.' Mike glanced round and looked, for a moment, at the hills beyond the church. 'They are coming up because they want what you have,' he said simply. 'This beautiful earth.'

For a moment, he looked enormously sad and again

something pricked in Jonah's mind. *I know I've seen him before,* he thought.

Mike paused as a clamour of disbelief broke out. 'Yes, I know. I know it sounds crazy but it is true, I'm afraid. And, by the way, the wolves you heard are a sort of demon, too.'

There were audible gasps of disbelief.

'But we must be able to get rid of the things!' an elderly man called from the middle of the churchyard.

Mike bit his lip. 'Not easy. The creatures here at Cascob aren't an isolated phenomenon, I'm afraid. I think many, many more of them will come to the surface in the Welsh Borders. They are blocking every single way of getting in touch with other places.'

'But how are they doing that?' asked the vicar.

'They are swarming over the local radio masts and communication installations, using a spell to cover all the telephone cables with some kind of fibre that traps the sound waves. A bit like silky spiders' webs. That's why you have no phones working. They want to isolate you, while more and more of them arrive.' He hesitated for a moment before saying reluctantly, 'Then they will attack in earnest.'

'What about the Army?' a woman called. 'Can't the things be shot?'

'What about explosives?' asked someone else.

Mike shook his head gravely. 'They are totally impervious to any modern weapon.'

A young man glared up at Mike, scowling. 'That's unbelievable, man! Are you standing there and telling us that we've fought in two world wars, not to mention Bosnia and Iraq and Afghanistan, but we can't get rid of these – animals and demons and things. It's pathetic!'

There were cries of agreement and shouts of anger. The Vicar of Knighton stood up. 'Please, everyone, let's keep calm,' he said, looking around. 'It's no use getting angry. If we are confronting the paranormal, ordinary weapons *won't* be of any use. The important thing is to keep our heads, and think how we can try to protect our community.'

'There is a way of destroying them,' Mike said, 'but it means you have to fight them face to face.' He looked around at the puzzled frowns. 'Face to face with a sword, I mean. I don't think many men today know how to fight like that, do they?

'There is no way I can soften this,' he added grimly. 'And I am deeply sorry to have brought you this terrible news. You *are* in danger. The Night Creatures don't want to share this world. They want to take it away! They don't want human beings on Earth – except as slaves.'

Mike bowed his head briefly and turned to talk to the Reverend Vaughan. As he did so, he glanced at the church and Jonah saw a shadow cross his face. Suddenly, a thought struck Jonah with such force that he nearly cried out.

'Erin,' he muttered. 'Come over here.'

He ran towards the wall at the back of the church, past the huddled knots of anxious villagers and pulled Erin behind a bush, so that nobody could see them.

'What's the matter?' Erin frowned at him.

'I don't want anyone else to hear this. They would just laugh at me. But the thing is, I was watching Mike and he turned and looked at the church, and something just came to me.' He swallowed. 'I think I might know who Mike is.'

Erin's eyes widened. 'Really? Not SAS, then?'

Jonah shook his head. 'First I need to explain something,' he said slowly. 'Something I didn't tell you about, after the wolf bit me.'

'Go on.'

'Well, I seemed to have a sort of nightmare. I was awake and everything, and the pain was terrible. I know I wasn't asleep. But I heard ghastly whispering voices and saw kind of nightmare faces and they chased me...' His voice shook and he faltered. 'I'm sorry. I don't mean to sound like a custard-head, but it was just awful.'

'*Custard*-head?'

'That's what we say at my school. You know, when someone's all scared about doing something they've got to.'

Erin leaned forward. 'It's OK, Jonah. You're no scaredy-cat. I was the one who cried, remember? And nothing so awful happened to me.'

He took a deep breath. 'Thanks.'

She looked puzzled. 'But what's that got to do with who Mike is?'

'Well, the same kind of thing happened, when I looked at Mike just now.' He laughed and waved his hands as Erin began to object. 'No, I don't mean I saw terrible things. The opposite, really. I looked at Mike just as he finished speaking and I seemed to see another Mike. Oh, gosh, it's so hard to explain.' He thumped the ground in frustration.

'Go on!'

'Well, when he looked at the church, I was thinking he looked really sad, and then, somehow, the sun shone on his hair, and it seemed to sort of blow back. But there's no wind, is there? And the air seemed to – sort of – shimmer.' Jonah was looking at her expectantly.

Erin sat back and wrinkled her nose. 'Were you – like – hallucinating?'

'No, I wasn't! Don't you see what I mean?'

She shook her head. 'No. Sorry,' she said slowly.

'Oh, Erin, you do! Think! Mike knows all about these strange things that are happening, the dragon and everything, but he hasn't said how he knows. He's sad when he looks at the church...'

'He just appears and we never know where from.' Erin put in, eagerly.

Jonah leaned forward and clutched her shoulders. 'And his name is Mike, which is short for...'

'Michael!' They both said it together. Erin's eyes were huge.

'It was what you said about him looking at the church,' she whispered. 'That's why he's here. It's his church, isn't it? You think he's Saint Michael the Dragonslayer.'

Chapter 13

ABRACADABRA

Jonah and Erin were still sitting by the churchyard wall, deep in discussion about Mike, when the screaming began. The children scrambled to their feet and peered round the bush.

'Oh, no, the Night Creatures are back. Look!' said Jonah, pointing. Six or seven grotesque little creatures were slithering over the roof or dangling from the guttering, taunting the appalled people down below.

'Oh, I don't like this!'

'Come on, then. Let's go back to the others,' said Jonah.

As they ran back to the church, Mike came racing away from the crowd, making towards the back of St. Michael's. As Mike turned the corner, the children saw Rhodri sprinting after him.

'I'll help you drive them off,' Rhodri called.

Mike stopped. 'No, mate. Thanks. Can you keep everyone together on the porch side though, and well away from the church? It will be safer.'

'Sure,' Rhodri said, and ran back up the path.

Erin bumped Jonah's arm. 'Mike's good at taking charge, isn't he?'

They exchanged glances.

The clergymen began to say The Lord's Prayer.

'Come on, everybody. Join in. Don't stop!' a man shouted. The vicar raised his voice and the villagers joined in, with all eyes fixed on the slates. The little fiends pranced in a mad pantomime, grimacing and hissing at them. Rhodri hurried to move people away.

'Get back,' he called, 'Get well away from the church, so these things can't touch you.'

The man who had run from the churchyard came hurrying back, panting for breath as he stumbled along. Under his arm he carried a shotgun.

'Good idea!' shouted one of his friends. 'Make space for Harry, everyone! We'll soon see if guns can't hurt them.'

The vicar looked round, saw Harry coming with his gun and waved his arms frantically.

'Tell him not to shoot,' he called urgently. 'Stop him, somebody. Stop him!'

People were moving quickly aside to let Harry aim his gun at the biggest fiend capering on the apex of the roof. Rhodri dashed towards him but before he could speak, the old man fired. There was a moment of terrible silence in the churchyard as they all looked up. The creature, motionless, stared down at them, its face contorted in rage. Then it shrieked and scampered down the church wall to the ground. It leaped across the grass, spitting and baring its teeth at the nearest people. They screamed and scattered, scrambling behind gravestones and bushes to get away.

As the children ran for the gate, one of Erin's schoolfriends stumbled over the edge of a grave that was hidden by long grass. She fell headlong onto the ground. The demon screeched with joy, bounded across the grass and leaped on her back. She squealed with terror and tried to roll over to knock it off. Before anyone could reach her, it clutched handfuls of her hair in its bony hands, yanked back her head and bit into her neck. She shrieked as blood poured from the wound, and then her body began to jerk violently.

'Megan, don't move!' Before Jonah could stop him, Erin's school friend Gethin flung himself on the Night Creature, trying to pull it off. It turned, grabbed his wrist and viciously sunk its teeth into his arm. Gethin grunted with pain and then he crumpled on to the grass. Like Megan, he began to twitch uncontrollably.

The scaly demon was sitting astride her back chortling, and raking its nails down her arms until they were a mass of bleeding scratches. She whimpered faintly as it kicked her hard with its bony heels but she seemed to be losing consciousness.

'Megan! Oh, my God, Megan!' A fair-haired woman raced across the churchyard, screaming, and had to be held back.

'Get off me,' she sobbed, as she struggled against the restraining hands. 'Let me go to my daughter!'

A woman put her arms round Megan's mother comfortingly, as the demon crowed with glee and leaped up and down on the girl's back. The Night Creatures on the roof hopped around, screeching with delight, as they watched. They jabbered at each other and then they all swung down from the porch and the guttering, bounded about among the squealing crowd and grabbed at people's clothes with their skinny little grey fingers. Children in the crowd screamed in panic and men were trying to push frightened women out of the way, as the grotesque little fiends herded them away from the gate and the wall that ran beside the lane.

Erin clutched Jonah's sleeve, as they stood wondering which way to run. Claire and Gwen peered from behind the huge yew tree. When they saw that there were no demons near the church porch, they rushed across the grass towards the children.

'Quick,' gasped Gwen. 'Slip away to the corner of the graveyard there, behind the church, and get over the wall into the field. Then we can run for home. You two go first. Quick now, before any of those things see you.'

'Yes, go on. Hurry,' urged Claire, giving Jonah a push. 'We'll be right behind you.'

Jonah took one last glance at the chaos among the gravestones. Through people's legs he could just make out Gethin, jerking on the ground. It reminded him how he shook, when the wolf had bitten him. Suddenly, he realised just what they had to do.

'Just a minute. I've got an idea.'

'No, Jonah. There's no time. We must get away while we can.' Claire took his shoulders and urged him towards the field wall. He twisted away from her.

'No, not yet. There's something we *have* to do.' He grabbed Erin's arm and pulled her along the path..

'*Jonah!* Come back!' Claire threw up her hands and the two women groaned with frustration.

At the corner of the church, he turned urgently to Erin. 'How does the spell work? What do you have to say?'

She looked puzzled for a second and then her eyes lit up. 'Oh, yeah. That's it! That'll get rid of them. Oh, brilliant, Jonah!' She bit her lip in thought. 'I think it goes...'

'That's no good,' Jonah interrupted. 'It's too chancy. If we don't say it right, it probably won't work. We'd better go in the church and learn it. Quick.'

'You do that. I'll get Mike. If he's who we think, he'll know how to use it.'

While Erin ran towards the back of the church, Jonah looked around to for Night Creatures. Seeing that there weren't any close to the church, he ran towards the south door. He peered over the gate into the porch and squinted up at its ceiling. The porch was empty. No fiends there.

'Jonah!' Erin was rushing back along the path. 'He's not there. Mike's not there. Did you see him come back?'

Jonah shook his head and scanned all the people backed behind the gravestones. 'He's not here. We'd be able to see him if he was. He's taller than most people.' He turned to Erin. 'What are we going to do?'

She bit her lip and then slapped her hand against her head. 'Oh, I'm dim! Of course. We need the vicar! *He'll* know it off by heart. Won't be a tick.' And she sprinted off across the grass, without looking to see where the Night Creatures were, and nearly colliding with Mr Vaughan, as the vicar hurried towards the church.

'Jonah's got an idea to frighten them off,' she burst out. 'The spell on the wall. It's to use against demons, isn't it?'

'Yes,' said the vicar, his face brightening. 'Well done! Quick. Come with me.'

'But— ' Erin waved towards Megan and Gethin.

'No, I can't just say the prayer. There's more to it than that,' gasped Mr Vaughan. 'You'll see in a minute.'

He seized Erin's arm and they ran towards the church door. Jonah was standing in the nave looking up at the framed explanation of the ancient spell, repeating it to himself. The vicar hurried into the vestry and came back with some sheets of paper and a couple of pens.

'What we have to do,' he said, carefully folding the paper, 'is copy out the *Abracadabra* spell.' He looked hard at Jonah. 'If you would help me, I won't have to waste precious time explaining to anyone else. But it might be dangerous.'

'Doesn't matter. I'll help,' Jonah blurted out. 'I'll be OK.'

'I will, too,' said Erin eagerly.

'Right,' said Mr Vaughan. 'Come and look.'

They went to stand in front of a framed explanation of the ancient spell. The word *Abracadabra* was written to make a triangle:

ABRACADABRA

ABRACADABR

ABRACADAB

ABRACADA

ABRACAD

ABRACA

ABRAC

ABRA

ABR

AB

A

'We need to copy it out exactly as it is on the wall,' the vicar explained, beginning to write, 'on five separate pieces of paper. We know that there was a terrible plague, in 1665 I think, and people wore the charm, folded up as an amulet. They had it round their necks to keep themselves safe against infection. We'll make amulets, too.' He stopped and thought for a moment. 'I don't think there's any string in the vestry, though. We'll have to find another way of hanging them round the children's necks.'

'Would it work if we fixed the charms to their clothing instead? Safety pins or paper clips?'

'I don't see why not. Good idea, Jonah. I know, we could use sticky tape. I think there's some in the cupboard in the vestry. Could you have a look, Erin?'

She nodded and shot off towards the vestry door. Mr Vaughan turned to Jonah. 'Then, and this is the dangerous bit, we have to somehow get past that creature and put them on the young people's clothes. We'll protect ourselves with them, too. Can you each write one out, while I do the others?'

Erin was soon back with a roll of tape. Working as fast and as neatly as they could, they wrote out the charms and stuck a long piece of tape to each one.

'Don't let the other end get stuck on the paper,' warned the vicar. 'Now, each of you put one on the front of your tee-shirt. So the demons can see them. That's right.'

In a few moments, they were running back towards the two unconscious children. The big demon kept rushing at the appalled group of people watching helplessly nearby and then sprang back to its victims. The other creatures crowed with joy as they made little shrieking dashes that scattered the crowd. Rhodri and Ted, armed with branches broken out of the hedge, were trying to drive the big one off but just as Mr Vaughan and the children ran up, it spat vile green phlegm into Ted's face. He gasped with pain and clawed at his eyes as the Night Creature grabbed Gethin by his ankle, digging its horny nails into his flesh until the blood ran, and began to tug him across the grass.

The onlookers scattered to make room as Mr Vaughan walked up to the demon, the spell taped to his shirt. He looked calm and determined. He and the Night Creature locked eyes for a second. Then, as it snarled and tensed to spring, Mr Vaughan's voice rang out across the churchyard, 'O Lord, we beseech thee for mercy. Grant that this holy charm ABRACADABRA may cure thy servants Megan and Gethin from all evil spirits and from all their diseases. Amen.'

The demon hissed and crouched possessively over Gethin, staring up at the vicar. Jonah seized his opportunity, while the creature was preoccupied, and moved quietly behind it. He lowered himself to the ground beside Megan carefully, hoping that he would not alert any of the other fiends. Then he tried to fasten the spell on her tee-shirt. It was awkward to stick it to the fabric and he was scared that the Night Creature would turn round and see what he was doing. It made his fingers feel clumsy. As he struggled to secure it properly, the demon turned and saw him. It screamed with rage and ran at him. Jonah jumped to his feet and held his own tee-shirt out, so that the creature could see the charm-paper.

'O Lord, we beseech thee for mercy,' he began. 'Grant – er – grant…' He began to falter but Mr Vaughan's strong voice joined in, 'Grant that this holy charm ABRACADABRA may cure thy servants Megan, Gethin and Jonah from all evil spirits and from all their diseases. Amen.'

As they repeated the prayer, a woman helped the vicar put a charm-paper on Gethin's shirt. The demon visibly shrank and began to gibber, covering its eyes with its clawed hands. The creature quailed and then lurched at the villagers. As they jumped out of its way, it raced back towards the drainpipe on the church wall, where it hung swearing and hissing with rage. Enraged and frustrated, the other little fiends scurried back to the church roof where they yowled and screamed abuse. The vicar looked down in distress at the two children on the ground, who were still jerking and shuddering. Megan's mother was on her knees, stroking Megan's cheek with trembling fingers.

'We need an ambulance!' she cried, looking up wildly.

'My husband's gone to bring up the Range Rover,' said a kindly-looking woman. 'Don't you worry. He'll have them over to Kington Hospital in a few minutes.'

A man and a red-haired woman edged through the crowd and bent over Gethin. The man looked over his shoulder at the anxious people around him. 'I think he's coming round,' he muttered. Gethin moaned faintly. His eyelids fluttered and he opened his eyes. At first, he stared upwards unblinkingly, as if he could not see. His mother gripped her husband's hand, biting her lip.

'Gethin,' said his father softly. 'We're here, son. You're going to be all right.' His voice trembled.

Then Gethin turned his head slightly and seemed to focus on his father's face. 'Dad,' he whispered groggily. He lay quietly for a moment and then his eyes opened wide, as his memory seemed to return. He reached out for his mother's hand. 'I saw terrible things,' he whispered in a frightened voice. 'I saw —' he faltered, as if he could not find the right words. He began to shake uncontrollably. Jonah gazed at him sympathetically. He guessed just what Gethin had seen.

The Reverend Vaughan joined the children and laid a hand on Jonah's arm. 'Well done, you two,' he said. 'That was quick thinking.'

The vicar's last words were drowned in an explosion of sound from beyond the wall. Then there was another immense roar and a great sheet of flame shot upwards from the woodland.

Chapter 14

THE AWAKENING

As tongues of fire streaked above the trees, the slates on the church seemed to shiver and billow. Suddenly, the roof was alive again with swarms of scrawny fiends, leaping over the slates, gibbering and squawking, and making lewd gestures at the horrified people. Everyone scrambled away from the church. A young man tapped Rhodri's arm.

'Don't look round too quickly,' Jonah heard him say in a low voice, 'but we are being surrounded.' He gave a slight nod towards the bushes overhanging the old wall separating Cascob churchyard from the hilly field on the western side of the church. Rhodri and Jonah followed his gaze and saw a couple of grey forms slide through the undergrowth. At the same time, they both caught a quick glimpse of a figure in a long, hooded robe, who slipped out of sight down the hill.

'Who was that?' asked Jonah. 'He's a bit brave!'

'Or bloody stupid,' said Rhodri. 'He'll get killed, if he's not careful.'

Erin let out a squeak and put her hands over her mouth.

'Looked like a monk,' said the other man, 'but I don't think it could have been. There's no monastery or anything round here.'

On the far side of the slope, another wolf loped away.

The man leaned over to mutter in Rhodri's ear. 'They're not real wolves, are they?'

'No. Like Mike said, they are demons,' Rhodri said. 'Oh, Duw, what next? This is awful. I can't see how we can get rid of them...'

As he raised his voice to be heard over the thunderous noise from the woods, a pearly radiance flickered in the east and began to grow in strength. Gradually, shining ribbons of light, gauzy rose and blue and soft gold, began to dance in the sky. The light shimmered, expanding and contracting, weaving across the sky in glowing folds. On the church, the demons howled in anger, hissing and spitting as they stared at the glimmering sky.

'Is it the *Aurora Borealis*?' someone gasped.

'The Northern Lights!' people were telling each other. 'It's the Northern Lights.'

Everyone looked up in wonder as the wavering light billowed above them, seeming now to advance and now recede. As the crowd gazed, they began to make out transparent shapes glowing in the pulsing colours.

'It's a message,' somebody said.

'No! Look!' Jonah was staring up in excitement. 'Look! It's not the Northern Lights. They are angels!' And he raised his arms to the sky, shouting with excitement.

The angels' vast wings beat gently in the streams of radiance. Their soft robes flowed around them and bright hair blew back from faces that had an unearthly beauty. Almost without being aware of what they were doing, the villagers began to kneel down, as they gazed upwards. The demons moaned as they cowered on the tiles. From the centre of the host of angels, a great winged form moved slowly earthward in a ring of light. The angel's luminous hair blew about his head and a huge golden scabbard was belted on to his billowing robe. Jonah was staring up at the being's face. His heart seemed to beat so hard, he felt as if his chest would burst.

'It's Mike, Erin! It's Mike. Look!' he shouted. But even then, he could hardly believe it was real. He turned to Erin, laughing in excitement. 'Mike *is* the Archangel! He *is* Saint Michael.' He shook her arm but she was rooted to the spot, staring at Mike with her mouth open. Jonah shook her again. He was almost dancing with excitement. 'Erin, he's the Dragonslayer! He's going to save us!'

The demons fled to the edge of the roof as the great angel

descended and hovered over the church. As the people gazed up at him, Erin groaned.

'Oh, no! Look at him. What's happened to him?'

With dismay, Jonah saw that the angel's hands and feet were skeletal, his great limbs frail and worn. As the young Mike Golding, he had looked strong and powerful but now the great Archangel appeared to be much older.

'Why is he looking so old?' Erin asked.

Jonah hesitated. 'Maybe it's like that bit in Peter Pan. You know. 'Do you believe in fairies?' If people don't believe in them, the fairies can't live on.'

'He's not a fairy!'

'I know *that*! I just meant perhaps it's the same with angels. Maybe *he'll* get stronger once people believe who he is.'

As Saint Michael came to hover above the church roof, a deafening roar, like the sound of a huge furnace, came from the west.

Flames shot above the earth until a curtain of fire and smoke screened the forest. There was a terrible cracking, tearing sound, and then Jonah heard an ear-splitting shriek over the noise of the roaring flames. There was a sound as if an army was pounding up the slope from the woods and, then, into the sky shot a gigantic winged shape, glowing red-bronze. Fire shot from its open mouth. Everybody screamed and threw themselves down on the ground. They lay there cowering, appalled, as the colossal beast seemed to block the sun.

Lazily, the Last Great Dragon of Wales swept about the sky above their heads, occasionally belching out tongues of flame. Hardly daring to look upwards through the smoke, Jonah and Erin could just see the light from the east glinting on its massive bronze scales and wicked claws. Around them, on the ground, everyone seemed paralysed with fear. Even the Night Creatures on the church were motionless and the wolves had stopped howling.

Frantically Jonah pulled Erin down behind a gravestone and they peered up into the billowing smoke. They could hardly see the angels. The choking clouds coming from the dragon's mouth had almost blotted out their glowing light. Jonah could feel Erin trembling and saw that his own hands were shaking, too. The dragon sailed up the valley and then, suddenly, it turned, raced back across the sky and whipped its great barbed tail about, striking viciously at the Archangel. Saint Michael swept out of range. His hands went to his scabbard and grimly he drew out the massive golden sword, but it seemed to the terrified onlookers that the angel was trembling with the strain.

The children's eyes never left the dragon, as it swirled about the sky. Without warning, it turned again and flew at Michael with a noise like a jet taking off, its terrible claws extended, flames pouring from its nostrils and gaping mouth. With shuddering effort, Michael raised the weapon above his head to strike, but he was hurled backwards by the wind of the roaring flames. The dragon streaked through the sky like a guided missile. Michael tried to slash...his fragile hands. The dragon flung itself away from the sword's arc and raced across the fields, whipping backwards and forwards across the hills.

'Look,' Erin whimpered, 'the demons are moving on the roof. Oh, Jonah, they're going to come down again! I don't think the spell will work on them all at once. They'll hurt us. And I 'm not sure Saint Michael *can* help now. We've got to get out of here!'

They grabbed each other's hand tightly, as the dragon turned and flew west, over the Radnor Forest.

'Wait till it's out of sight. When nothing is looking this way,' Jonah muttered, 'we'll run for it! Wait till I say "go" and then run as fast as you can. OK?'

Erin nodded and squeezed his hand. They were crouching, tense and ready to run, when they heard a scraping sound and a huge grey wolf bounded on to the churchyard wall. Jonah winced as Erin's fingers dug into him. More wolves with glaring yellow eyes slunk up and down the field. Sobbing with fright, people scrambled away from the church. The sky darkened again and smoke obscured the angelic radiance completely. A gigantic booming noise reverberated around the Radnor hills. The Last Great Dragon of Wales was laughing.

Chapter 15

ALPHA MALE

As the dragon circled the Forest again and the terrible laughter died away, pandemonium broke out. The crowd pelted towards the lych-gate, everyone struggling to push through. The wolves, snarling as they saw their prey beginning to escape, raced up and down beside the churchyard wall to find crumbling places where they could scramble over. Jonah pulled Erin to her feet.

'Come on! No, not towards the gate.' He dragged her away from the crowd.

'Jonah!' Erin gasped. 'It's the wrong direction! We want to go the other way!'

'No. The lane'll be too full. We shan't be able to run.' He jerked his head towards the gate where men and women, coughing in the dragon's smoke, were jostling frantically to get through. Some clambered over the wall beside the gate into the lane, others shouted for help with elderly relatives. Two huge wolves began to creep towards the edge of the crowd. Men started yelling and panicking, throwing clods of earth at them. A couple of clergymen, looking over their shoulders, swiftly helped to lift the smallest children over the wall to the lane.

'See?' Jonah panted. They raced towards the far corner of the churchyard wall, above the lane.

'Let's get over the wall here and then across the lane into the fields. We can go quicker that way.'

There was a sudden burst of gunfire. The children both jumped and turned to see that all the wolves had got into the churchyard. They crouched at bay, red tongues lolling. The noise of Harry's shotgun had stopped them in their tracks but, of course, the gun could not injure them. It was only a matter of seconds, Jonah knew, before the creatures realised that the gun held no threat. Erin turned towards the wall again but Jonah gripped her hand.

'Don't move,' he whispered urgently. 'If we run, they'll notice us. They'll go for us then.'

The Reverend Vaughan suddenly dashed out of the church and strode calmly in front of old Harry, holding a copy of the *Abracadabra* spell towards the wolves. The farmer stood shakily clutching his gun, as the wolves, snarling, backed away. The big pack leader ran up and down, trying to cross the invisible barrier the vicar was making. Unable to find a way to leap at their prey, the wolves whined with frustration and Harry grinned.

Something made Jonah look up, and he gasped. The Archangel was standing on the church roof, searching the sky. 'Look at Saint Michael. He looks much more like Mike now.'

'He's getting stronger,' Erin murmured.

'Everyone's been praying. Perhaps it's helping him,' Jonah whispered back.

Above the church, the sky seemed to waver and glow. Then the radiance crackled, as if the air were splintering into fragments of golden glass. The light was so bright that the children had to cover their eyes and look down. Above them, something flashed, and then there was a piercing shriek. A Night Creature dropped to the ground, and for a moment lay motionless across a grave. It looked as if it was carved from stone. Then the body cracked into tiny fragments and a wisp of shadow blew away from it, swirling in the air towards the woods. The children, squinting through their fingers, saw two angels standing astride the roof, hacking at the squealing fiends as they scuttled to get away. Their great wings stirred as they skimmed over the tiles and their swords gleamed as another loathsome creature was dispatched. Beyond the church, Saint Michael was driving a couple of wolves out of the churchyard. They growled and snapped at him, leaping aside to avoid the sharp edge of his sword.

'Why doesn't he kill them?' Erin asked in a low voice.

'I dunno. But look how fast they move!'

The rest of the wolf pack, disheartened, had given up trying to break through the barrier of the charm and slunk away over the churchyard wall. Jonah, watching them go, caught sight of the shadowy, cloaked figure standing in the shade of a tree. He scrambled to his feet but when he looked again, there was nothing beneath the branches after all. He screwed his eyes up, blinking, but he couldn't see anyone in the meadow. As the wolves loped towards the forest, he caught a glimpse of what looked like smaller creatures moving with them. Some demons had got away, then, and it looked as if they and the wolves were making for the fissure. Perhaps the angels would drive them all away from Cascob and back into the Underworld. He turned to look for the Archangel again and froze, gripping Erin's arm.

The largest wolf, the alpha male which had attacked him the day before, was standing a few feet away, its yellow eyes fixed on Jonah. Saliva dripped from its jaws. It took a slow step forward, and then another, drawing its lips back from its fangs in a rumbling snarl. Jonah could not move; he felt as if his body had turned to ice. He could hear Erin breathing shakily behind him.

The wolf brought one foot slowly forward, hunched its shoulders and then erupted into a streak of snarling fur. It slammed into Jonah, knocking him and Erin backwards. Everything seemed to go into slow motion. He felt the weight of its feet pressing down on his chest and legs. Its stinking breath made him gag. He tensed for the terrible ripping bite, but it did not come. Instead, there was a high-pitched scream, a smell of burning hair and a flash of golden light. He felt the rush of wings, and then he was being lifted up and swept gently across the churchyard. An angel lowered him to the grass. He began to tremble as he watched Erin getting to her feet. Another angel was hovering above her, protectively. Near the lych gate, two more angels pursued the wolf, which scrabbled over the wall and disappeared.

'You are safe now,' said the one who had rescued him. 'Stay here while we chase off the others.'

Two angels floated over the church, searching in case any fiend were still hiding behind the guttering. Another searched the churchyard and two more bent over Megan and Gethin, who were both sitting up. They had nasty wounds and blood all over their clothes but they were conscious again, and talking. A couple of other angels, in the hill-meadows beyond the church wall, examined the hedgerows and looked along the lane. Once the wolves had been driven off, people stopped trying to rush out of the churchyard and were spellbound by the sight of the heavenly beings. The villagers began to feel that the angels would somehow keep them safe from the Red Dragon, if it returned.

Jonah sighed with relief and shakily began to stand up. He looked towards the hills, wondering where the dragon was. He soon found out.

Chapter 16

TALKING TO A DRAGON

The sky darkened again, and the oppressive gloom seemed to stop the villagers in their tracks. The angelic light above the church faded. Abruptly, total silence fell. No one seemed able to move. Too scared to speak, everyone stared upwards as the enormous bulk of the dragon loomed again in the sky.

Gazing down at Michael, who swept down to stand astride the roof ridge, the dragon rumbled. Jonah got a distinct impression that it was talking to the Archangel. Though the crackling noise of its breath made the words indistinct, Jonah thought he heard it say, 'The sword gets heavier with the passing years, does it not, Michael?'

Jonah gripped Erin's arm in excitement. 'Listen to that!'

Erin looked confused. 'What?'

But Jonah had turned back to concentrate on what the dragon was saying. It swished its tail savagely, as it moved above the church.

'For a thousand years and more, you have locked me beneath the earth. Is it not enough? Can I not taste some freedom before you come back to my forest to fight me again? *My* forest, Michael. *My* land, not yours. *My* beautiful Wales.'

Michael rose into the air until he was level with the dragon's head. His hair blew about his face in the wind of its breath and he looked angry, as he began to speak. Jonah could just make out something that sounded like: 'Ferny, Ferny, what have you done? You sent fire through the caverns and opened the eyes of the dwellers in the Underworld. Now the Night Creatures are loose, bringing Evil here.'

The dragon let out a spurt of flame. 'I awoke. That is all. Do not blame me if the demons seize an opportunity. We dragons do not deal with their kind.'

The Archangel looked grim. 'I do not come to kill you. But you must leave.'

'What?' The dragon's roar made all the villagers cringe.

Saint Michael soared into the air and swept towards the creature. 'More than a thousand years have passed, as you said. The world you knew has gone. The people here have never seen a dragon before. But they know of you, the Last Great Dragon of Wales. They place your image on their buildings; they think of you with pride.'

The dragon cocked its head on one side and looked at the angel thoughtfully.

'They are proud of their Red Dragon, Ferny. Do not hurt them. Leave them in peace. Then you and I need not fight again.'

'We-ell...' The dragon's mood seemed to have softened. It moved lazily above the valley, lowering its head to peer down at the throng of people in the churchyard and the lane beyond. 'But I am hungry,' it said in a voice that sounded like roaring flames to the frightened people below. 'Very hungry.'

Michael gripped the sword. 'No, Ferny. Do no evil here!'

The dragon squeezed its eyes shut. Jonah thought it was amused. 'Well, I'm too hungry to want to fight you. No Welshmen then. But there are some delicious-looking cattle down there.'

Cattle! Oh, no! Without thinking, Jonah bolted forwards. Panicking, he yelled up at the dragon.

'No! No! Don't kill the cattle. Please don't! They're my uncle's.' He had his head flung back, staring up at the dragon. 'They're prize Herefords!' *Oh, you idiot! As if the dragon would care about that.* Then he had a brain-wave. 'We can get you meat!' he called. 'We can get you all you want from the butcher's shop.'

Michael and the dragon hovered above the church, gazing down at him with surprise. Jonah felt surprised, himself.

Appalled, even. He hadn't thought about what he was going to say; the words had just spilled out. He wondered what would happen if nobody wanted to pay for meat for the dragon. What would happen if it ate everything in the butcher's shop? Oh, Hell's teeth, what had he done? He turned slowly round to look for Bryn and found everyone's eyes on him. He noticed one of the villagers nudge another one and nod his head, smirking a bit. Jonah realised people thought he was crazy to shout at the dragon.

But then, it circled and lost height, dropping down to the meadow. Immediately, everyone stopped looking at Jonah and stood mesmerised by fear of the huge creature in the field. The dragon was swishing its tail over the damp grass and peering across the lane. Then its small amber eyes fastened on Jonah. He gulped and looked round frantically for help but everyone was standing stock still, hardly daring to breathe. Jonah looked apprehensively at the dragon. It was still looking hard at him but, somehow, it didn't look as if it was about to attack. Its gaze was interested, you could almost say friendly. It raised its horned head to look up at Saint Michael on the church roof.

'Who is the young Heart Eater? Did he speak the truth? Will they bring me meat? I'm ravenous. I could eat the entire herd over there.' It jerked its head towards the farms down the lane.

'Be patient for a little while. I have something to explain to the boy first.'

The dragon groaned but dropped down meekly enough on to the grass, settling itself to rest. The crowd in the churchyard gazed at it, open-mouthed, and Jonah began to look for Bryn. Surely he would know how to get some meat for it. Emlyn and Gwen came hurrying over, and Erin, with Gethin and some more friends, rushed towards him.

'Are you all right, son?' Emlyn asked, gripping his shoulder.

Gwen looked anxious. 'I don't like the way that great thing keeps staring at you! What's going on, Jonah?'

'I don't really know,' he began, as Bryn and Claire joined them.

'Whatever did you shout like that for? It was awfully dangerous, love,' said Claire. 'It might have gone for you.'

Bryn shook his head at her. 'It's OK. No harm done.'

'Saint Michael's over the moon about something,' Emlyn put in, nodding towards the Archangel, who was chatting animatedly with the dragon.

'It's because Jonah yelled at the dragon,' Gethin said.

'Hardly likely,' another boy said. 'If you ask me, it was daft to copy the noise it makes, like he did.' He turned to Jonah. 'No offence or anything, but if it had got mad, that old thing could have just gobbled you up. Nice snack for it you'd be.'

Erin rounded on him. 'He *wasn't* copying it. Were you, Jonah?'

'No, course not. It wanted to eat Bryn's cattle and I just said I'd try and get it some meat.'

Bryn's eyes were wide. 'You what?'

Everyone gaped at Jonah.

Saint Michael had crossed the lane and began to laugh. 'You should just see your faces!' His smile made them feel as if they were standing in warm sunshine. 'You heard Jonah talking to the dragon, didn't you?'

The children looked at each other. 'We heard him yelling at it,' Gethin said uncertainly, not wanting to seem rude.

'Oh, it was rather more than just shouting.' Michael said. 'And did you notice how the dragon calmed down afterwards? Well, it's because of Jonah.'

As everybody swung round in surprise to look at him, he scuffled his feet on the grass and flushed with embarrassment.

Michael went on, 'I've discovered something wonderful about Jonah. I'm just going to tell everybody what I've found out.'

'What's he done?'

'It's not what he's done but what he's going to do,' said Saint Michael. 'Everything is going to be fine because *Jonah can control the dragon!'* With a slight movement of his wings, he rose above the wall and dropped lightly into the churchyard. The Archangel's face was radiant. He looked even younger now, much more like his Mike Golding self. He stretched out his hand, shimmering with light, towards Jonah.

'I wondered whether I dared hope for this,' he said, smiling. 'Jonah, this is marvellous!'

Jonah turned apologetically to the Archangel. 'I know I shouldn't have said anything. It just sort of came out. I hope I haven't mucked everything up – um – Sir,' he finished lamely.

Michael laughed and the sound made Jonah feel warm. 'Hey, you can still call me Mike! No, it was not *what* you said, though it is a good idea. No, I am overjoyed because you said anything at all. Really! Look at the dragon. He doesn't look angry, does he?'

Jonah looked. It was true. The dragon did seem quite peaceful, stretched out over the meadow, with sunlight burnishing his scaly hide. 'Erm – I hope it's OK,' he said. 'About feeding it, I mean. You could get some meat, Bryn, couldn't you?' He bit his lip, staring anxiously at his uncle.

Bryn looked across at the dragon. 'Phew! Bit of a tall order, son. It'll eat a helluva lot, won't it?' He turned to Saint Michael. 'Please, what did you mean, about Jonah being able to control it? We don't understand.'

'Ask yourselves,' said the Archangel, 'why Jonah suddenly shouted at the dragon.' He looked round at the puzzled faces. 'He shouted because he knew what the dragon wanted. He *understood* what the dragon was saying.' He laughed. 'Come to that, none of you could understand the sounds Jonah was making either. Don't you see, everyone? Jonah is the only person, apart from we angels, who *knew* what the dragon said. Jonah, and possibly *only* Jonah among human beings, can talk to him.' The Archangel put out a hand. 'In a moment, I'll go and explain to everyone else, but I think you and your family and friends should know first, Jonah. So gather round. I have something amazing to tell you.'

Chapter 17

DRAGONS AND MASTERS

As he looked up at Michael, Jonah could hear lots of whispering. He couldn't look for long though, because the radiance that flowed from the angel's robes was so bright that it almost made his eyes water. He thought how strange everything had suddenly become. He imagined calling his parents when they could use the phones again. 'Hi, Mum and Dad. I've just been talking to an angel and there is a dragon in the field by the church.'

'Mike,' Jonah began, hesitantly. It was no good; he simply could not call this awesome being by such an ordinary name. 'Er – Michael, can I ask you something?'

'Of course.'

'How come the last *Welsh* dragon speaks English?'

The Archangel chuckled. 'He doesn't.'

Jonah looked up in puzzlement. 'But I spoke English to him!'

'No, you didn't!' Gethin cried.

Michael smiled. 'Jonah thought he did.'

Jonah frowned. 'But – how can a *dragon* understand what I'm saying, anyway? I don't get it.'

'I know. I'm sure none of you do, so let me try to explain. When I first met you, Jonah,' the Archangel said, 'I hardly dared to hope that your name meant what I wanted it to mean.'

'*Jonah*?'

'No, your surname. Drake. Do you know what it signifies?'

Jonah shook his head thoughtfully. 'I expect my ancestors bred ducks or hunted for them, or something like that.' He looked at Michael. 'I hate being called Drake,' he added wryly.

'Jonah Quack-quack? Ducky Drake?' suggested Gethin.

'You've got it! When I won the Year Eight football prize, they

87

all quacked when my name was called out.'

'His dad's school nickname was Aylesbury,' Claire put in.

Michael grinned. 'You will be the one who is laughing now, Jonah. In your family's case, the name has nothing to do with ducks. You have just proved that!'

Jonah was looking totally mystified. 'How?'

'Do you know any Latin?'

'Only a few words. I could start Latin next term, if I wanted to, but I think I'll probably go for Spanish.'

'Well, you might like to know this bit of Latin. The name Drake is an old English surname and comes originally from the Latin word *Draco*. That means "dragon".'

'Really? I never knew that!' Jonah tried to suppress a grin of pleasure.

'Well I never!' said Gwen.

Michael went on, 'From ancient times the name *Dragon*, in any language, was borne by men who had a special bond with the dragon races. If a warrior fought with a dragon and killed it, there would be a feast in his honour and he would be given the dragon's heart to eat.'

'Yuk!'

Michael grinned at the children's disgusted faces. 'Ah, but there was a reason for this strange practice. Er – how can I explain? When the men who had killed the dragons digested the hearts and blood, they showed dragon-like *qualities*. They had dragon spirit, as it were, so there was a special bond between the Heart Eaters and dragons. A human being had to be very brave and very skilled indeed to overpower a dragon, and the beasts knew it. They respected those men.

'After he'd eaten, the hero could understand and speak all the dragon languages. But, what's more – and this is really important – they would obey him, because they admired him. Do you begin to see what I'm saying?'

Jonah shook his head slowly. *Surely the Archangel wasn't*

suggesting that he could have eaten a dragon's heart.

Michael laughed at his bewildered expression. 'Bear with me a little. The thing is, they could pass on the gift to their sons and grandsons.'

Claire's mouth dropped open. 'Are you saying Jonah's one of them? That someone in his dad's family fought a dragon once?'

'Yes, I am.'

Jonah was stunned. Saint Michael patted his shoulder. 'Hard to take in, isn't it? It's true, though. Anyway, let me go on with the story. As the dragons withdrew to their caverns underground, men began to think of them as legendary creatures. The people who were born with the ability to understand and control them rarely saw a dragon any more. Eventually, most people forgot about the family gift. Very few people realised it had ever existed.

'But Jonah just proved that the power *is* still being passed on, even though people like him, who possess it, may not be aware of it. Maybe it has jumped a generation or two, maybe it has leaped over many generations. But the line of descent, however obscure, is unbroken.' He looked round gravely. 'He is the living proof. You are descended from such a line, Jonah. One of your ancestors must have been a great hero, a Heart Eater. That makes you a Dragoneer.'

Jonah, beside him, looked as if he'd been punched hard in the head and everyone else looked mystified.

Saint Michael laughed. 'You really should see your faces!'

Emlyn was frowning. 'What I don't understand is this. If Jonah, who's just a boy – and I accept he's special and all that – but if he can get the dragon to obey him, well, you're an angel, Mike – er, Michael. Surely, it would be safer, if you told it what to do, wouldn't it?'

'*Dad!*' Erin rolled her eyes. 'Mike's explained all about Jonah's ancestor eating a dragon's heart.'

'Yes, I know but—'

'Oh, Dad! Just think. Angels *don't eat meat.*'

Gwen tutted. 'Erin!'

Erin looked apologetically at Emlyn. 'Sorry. I didn't mean it to sound the way it came out.' She brightened. 'Come to think of it, I don't suppose angels have ancestors, either.'

Gwen looked round at the adults with a 'What can you do?' gesture, while they all tried not to laugh. Jonah could see Michael was stifling a grin.

'It is true,' he said, 'that I and my kind don't consume flesh. We cannot take dragon spirit into ourselves, cannot bond with the dragon races in the way the Heart Eaters did. Dragons fear and distrust our power in battle, because we have fought and killed so many. Dragons see angels as formidable enemies.'

The Archangel looked ruefully at the group of wondering villagers. 'I doubt the dragon would ever trust me, as he will surely trust Jonah. Well,' he said, 'I'd better go and tell all your neighbours.'

He walked towards the church. Exchanging looks, the children followed him and listened with growing excitement as the Archangel began to tell all the villagers about Jonah and his ancestors.

'Now you are safe. You needn't be afraid of the dragon any longer,' he finished.

'But that's only a boy,' an elderly man objected. 'How can a young chap like him control a darned great thing like that? He'd be but a mouthful for it!'

The Reverend Vaughan also looked dubious. 'Forgive me for seeming to doubt,' he said gravely to the angel, 'but how could Jonah possibly make the dragon do what he wants? It seems quiet now but think of the devastating amount of damage it can do, if it becomes angry – or just hungry. How can we believe that young Jonah can stop it from killing us all?'

Saint Michael looked amused. 'I think most people in the Radnor Forest found it hard to believe in *my* existence until this morning,' he said gently, and held up his hands as a clamour of apology and denial broke out. 'But I do understand. Naturally, it is difficult for you to believe that the dragon will obey Jonah Drake. It's hard for Jonah!' The Archangel looked sympathetically at all the people. 'I understand your doubts,' he said. 'Of course I do. But even though he was unaware of it, Jonah was born with this power. And now we'll prove it to you!' He turned and beckoned Jonah forward. 'He is going to show you, aren't you, Jonah? He's going to go over and command the dragon.'

Jonah's knees felt wobbly and there were a thousand butterflies tumbling around in his stomach. He had never felt so scared. What if the dragon got angry and burned him? Worse still, what if it tried to eat him? He looked at the Archangel apprehensively. Would Michael be able to save him if something went wrong?

He swallowed hard. 'Yes,' he croaked. 'I'll have a go.'

The church ministers were shaking their heads and Bryn looked appalled.

'Sir,' he remonstrated, striding over to the Archangel. 'With great respect, we can't put someone as young as Jonah in a situation where he might be killed!'

There was a cry of protest from somewhere in the crowd and Claire pushed through, followed by the Morgans and Rhodri.

'Saint Michael, please listen to my husband.' Claire was wild-eyed. 'I'm sorry, but please don't ask me to let Jonah do this. He is my responsibility while he's staying with us. How would I face his parents, if anything happened to him?'

Bryn looked at the Archangel sombrely. 'Forgive us, my lord, but my wife is right. Jonah shouldn't face the dragon. He is still a child.'

'Bryn!' Jonah flushed. A child! As if! He'd be a teenager in a few weeks! Even though he was frightened, he didn't want everyone to see how nervous he felt, and he certainly didn't want to let Saint Michael down. 'I'll be all right,' he muttered to Claire, but even to himself his voice sounded small and shaky.

Now Rhodri stepped forward. 'Sir, I used to be a soldier. Let me have a go. If the worst happened, well, I'm not married now. I haven't any children. If anything should go wrong, it would be better that it happened to me and not to Jonah.'

Michael smiled at him. 'That's a brave offer. But you are not descended from the Families of Domination. You *cannot* command the dragon. If Jonah's father were here, it is possible that he could. But he's not here, so it seems only Jonah has the power.' He looked around at Claire and Bryn kindly. 'Have no fear for Jonah. The dragon *will* obey him. Watch, and you'll see.'

Claire's mouth trembled and she looked near to tears but she daren't argue with the great Archangel.

Michael turned and touched Jonah lightly on the arm. The spot he touched seemed to glow with warmth and immediately Jonah felt better; the butterflies subsided and he felt quite calm and determined.

'Come on, we will go back across the lane.'

'How shall I get him to come to me?'

'Just call him by his name. From now on, wherever he is, he will hear you.'

'Michael, what did you call him? It sounded like "Ferny".'

'His name is Ffyrnig – *wild as a furnace*.' The Archangel spelt it out.

'Is it all right to call him that? It's not too casual, is it?' Jonah felt anxious as they went out of the churchyard. 'I mean, he's so important – the Last Great Dragon of Wales and all that. Ought I to say 'my lord' or something? Won't he think I'm being a bit, like, pushy?'

The Archangel began to laugh. 'Jonah, you have to realise that however mighty Ffyrnig seems, from now on *you* will be much more important. You can make him obey you; *he* won't be able to control *you*.'

'But he's *huge*. I still don't see how I can possibly make him do anything he doesn't want to.'

Michael gripped Jonah's shoulders. 'Well, if you look steadfastly into Ffyrnig's eyes, and tell him with all your heart and will what you want him to do, he will obey. There's a bond between the dragons and families like yours, Jonah. He will be bound by your will as a Master Dragoneer and, what is more, it will seem to him the right thing to do.'

'What shall I ask him to do?'

'Oh, just tell him to stand up and walk round the field with you. That will be enough to show everyone you're in charge.'

Jonah scrambled over the gate into the meadow and the angel, alighting on the grass beside him, looked deeply into his eyes. 'He must feel your truth and goodness, Jonah. It is through you that Ffyrnig will learn to tell good deeds from bad ones. That is why you must never lie to him and you must never, never tell him to do anything you know to be wrong. For if you do, you will unleash a terrible evil on the world, and your power over the dragon will weaken.'

Jonah gazed up at the Archangel. As he looked into Michael's eyes, he felt as if golden light was running through his veins. Suddenly, he felt excited and proud and ready for any challenge. 'I will do my best,' he said. 'I promise.'

Chapter 18

MY NAME IS JONAH DRAKE

The Great Dragon opened its eyes and squinted as Jonah walked out into the meadow. Everyone was tense with apprehension. Jonah stared up at the dragon's huge frame and the dragon looked back at him expectantly. Jonah turned to Michael, who was still standing by the hedge. The Archangel nodded reassuringly and Jonah, aware of all the eyes focused on him, held his head high and walked forward another few steps. His legs began to feel horribly wobbly and his mouth was dry. He stopped a few yards away, hoping that he could dodge backwards if the beast blew flames at him.

'You need not be afraid of my breath, Master,' said Ffyrnig mildly. 'I only breathe out fire when I need to.'

'I didn't say anything!' Jonah stuttered.

'Your eyes did,' remarked the dragon. His own eyes were twinkling with humour. He settled more comfortably on the grass and folded his enormous, bat-like wings over his body. There was a long sigh from the watching crowd.

Jonah's eyes had widened with surprise but he felt amused, as well. 'I can see I shan't be able to tell *you* any porkies.'

The dragon's eyes snapped open and he turned his great head expectantly. 'Pork? On the contrary, I should love you to talk about it. Have they brought me some?'

'Oh, not yet.' Jonah groaned and banged his forehead. 'I need to get you some meat, don't I? I should have asked someone.'

The dragon blew out a little smoke. 'I could murder a cow,' he said.

Jonah shot him a glance and drew himself up. He tried to speak firmly. 'My name is Jonah Drake,' he began, trying to sound confident. 'Saint Michael says that I am a Dragoneer. He would like you to walk across the field with me. Just for a moment or two, and then we'll get you something to eat.'

The dragon looked doubtful.

He's going to refuse, Jonah thought, beginning to feel panicky. Then an idea, as if someone had switched on a light bulb, popped into his head. 'Just to show all the people how magnificent you are,' he coaxed.

The dragon sighed deeply and rose majestically to his feet. Excited gasps and low cheers came from the churchyard. The dragon squeezed his eyes together in a way that seemed to show he was pleased. As they walked across the meadow, Jonah looked up at the scaly head, high above his own, and thought how magnificent the dragon really was. Tentatively, he put his hand against the warm, shining scales on the dragon's side. He found it hard to believe that he was walking beside a real, live dragon. He didn't want the moment to end.

But Ffyrnig needed feeding. Jonah stopped and looked up. 'If you wait here in the field, I'll go and ask my uncle to bring you some meat.'

'Yes, Master,' rumbled the dragon. 'Will it take long? I am ravenous.'

Jonah bit his lip, acutely aware that he had to be absolutely truthful. 'I honestly don't know. Someone has to go to the butcher's shop in Knighton and I'm not sure what time it opens. But they will be as quick as they can. Look, I'll go and see if my aunt has any meat in the freezer.' He looked searchingly at the dragon, who had sunk on to the grass with a dejected expression. 'You could just nibble on whatever we can find, till your real meal arrives. OK?'

Ffyrnig brightened. 'Thank you. I'm afraid I shouldn't have flown up and down the valley, so soon after waking up. I feel quite weak.'

Which was a good thing, Jonah thought, as he ran back to

Michael. 'He needs a meal quickly,' he said. 'I think Claire has some chops and things in the freezer that Ffyrnig could eat, while someone goes to the butcher. Shall I go and sort it out?'

The Archangel nodded and then he smiled. 'I should leave you now. We are needed in Hereford. There seems to be trouble there, too. '

Jonah immediately felt anxious. 'Do you have to go? What about the wolves?'

'Yes, the wolves—' Saint Michael began and then checked himself, looking gravely at Jonah. 'Well, we must talk about them when there is more time. For now, the people in the Forest need not worry too much about them. Demons fear the power of those dragons that serve man. They know the dragons' breath can wipe them from your world. If they come up through the fissure in the woods again, tell Ffyrnig to drive them back to the Underworld.'

'Will he really do that, if I ask?'

Michael nodded. 'Of course. Trust your power, Jonah, and don't look so worried. Ffyrnig recognised what you are straightaway. Otherwise, he wouldn't be lying there so quietly, I can tell you!'

Jonah still felt a bit doubtful.

'Hereford's not very far, is it?'

Michael laughed. 'No, it's not many miles away. It looks as if the Night Creatures may be starting to gather around the cathedral.'

'More of them? Is it because of Ffyrnig?'

'Maybe. The heat he generated may have roused more demons. Anyway, it seems that some strange creatures have been seen in Cathedral Green, and the local people are frightened. Be brave, Jonah. My fellows and I must go now.'

Jonah looked up at the great Archangel and, for a moment, their eyes met. Again he had the sensation of golden light running through his veins and instantly felt happy again, and confident and brave. Then the light around Michael grew so bright that Jonah had to cover his eyes, and when he could open them again, the angels had gone. He climbed over the gate into the lane and ran back to the crowded churchyard. Claire rushed up to hug him, and a crowd of people immediately surrounded him, but quietly, in case they disturbed the dragon. Everyone spoke in low voices, asking if he was all right and wanting to know where the angels were.

'OK. OK.' He was laughing and breathless, as everybody crowded round to hear what he had to say.

Rhodri put his arm round Jonah. 'Make way, everyone, please. Let the boy have some room. Here, stand on this.' He swung Jonah up on to a flat tombstone and looked round for the Reverend Vaughan. 'No disrespect to the dead, Mr Vaughan, but I think everybody should hear what the boy has to say.'

'Quite right,' said the vicar. 'Can you be quiet, everyone, please? Let Jonah speak.'

The whispering died down. Jonah looked round at the crowd and grinned when he found Erin beaming up at him. 'First,' he said, speaking as loudly as he could, 'we should get some meat to the dragon. He hasn't eaten for so long that he's feeling weak.'

'Good thing too,' shouted the old farmer, Harry. 'We don't want to be feeding that thing up.'

There were cheers and cries of 'Yeah, that's right. Good old Harry.' Then lots of hushing, and meaningful glances at the meadow.

'No!' Jonah raised his voice again. 'If we don't feed him, *he'll find his own food.*' He looked around, pleased. *That had shut everyone up.* He went on: 'Saint Michael says the dragon will do what we want now and he will keep the demons away. He says the demons know that some dragons serve us humans, so the Night Creatures are frightened of them. With any luck, the wolves will stay out of the dragon's way, too.' He took a deep breath and looked around, as there was a buzz of relief. 'So, the most important thing is to get him some food. Please, has anyone got some meat he could have, just until we can get him a real meal from the butcher? By the way, his name is Ffyrnig. I think that's F-f-y-r-n-i-g.'

Several people called out that they had meat at home they could bring.

'It will take a few minutes to defrost, mind,' called one woman in the crowd.

'I don't think that brute will worry about your chops being frozen, Joan,' chuckled Mr Morgan. 'He's got a better built-in defroster than your microwave!'

There was a shout of laughter. A farmer, who turned out to be the chairman of the Parish Council, suggested that the parish could provide funding for a good feed for the dragon. As there were enough parish councillors in the churchyard to take a vote, they agreed, and the chairman offered to drive to the butcher's shop in Knighton. The Reverend Vaughan suggested that it was time for everyone to go home, but to take great care, just in case any of the wolves managed to slip past the dragon. Children must on no account be outside on their own, he said.

But now that the great danger had passed, everyone seemed reluctant to leave. People wanted to talk about the incredible things they had just seen. Who would have thought, they said to each other, that when they got out of bed this morning, on a perfectly ordinary summer's day, that by half-past-eight they would have seen demons and a dragon and shining angels? They couldn't wait to tell all their friends, when they could use their phones again.

Chapter 19

FEEDING FFYRNIG

Nobody could take their eyes off Ffyrnig. They kept peering at him over the churchyard wall. When Claire and Gwen came running back up the lane, each carrying large bags of frozen meat, people started to trickle into the road, feeling brave enough now to come and gaze over the hedge into the meadow.

'Here we are,' Gwen puffed. 'Whew, that was heavy.'

Emlyn took her bags and then Claire's, heaving them over the wall, and Jonah tipped the frozen parcels of meat on to the grass. The dragon immediately rose to his feet and took a step nearer. Jonah turned round quickly.

'Stay where you are, Ffyrnig. You'll frighten everybody. I'll bring your food over.' He started to unwrap a big pack of chops. Erin was with some of her school friends whom she hadn't seen since the end of term. They had come to hang over the gate and Jonah smiled up at them. Then he realised they were all giggling and he felt himself beginning to blush. He knew he must look funny, hissing at a dragon.

'That's so weird,' said a girl who was leaning on the gate beside Erin. 'Did you know your friend could do totally freaky things?'

Jonah's insides swelled with indignation. He wasn't some kind of sideshow! He turned away and pretended he had not heard. Perhaps he ought to be quiet and let Ffyrnig do whatever he wanted. If the dragon started chomping away on that girl and her friends, she would be begging Jonah to talk to him!

The girl's voice carried clearly. 'How can he possibly understand what a dragon, an *animal*, is saying? It's not normal.' She lowered her voice but Jonah still heard her. 'Maybe he's possessed! Like that Elizabeth Lloyd was.'

'He is not!' Erin was furious.

'Nonsense, Amy! Of course he's not,' said a man's voice loudly. Jonah looked up. Several older people had come to stand behind the children and a middle-aged man in a sports jacket was shaking his head at Erin's friend. 'No, it's not freaky at all, as it happens. Didn't you listen to Saint Michael? You should be careful what you say. You can hurt people's feelings with comments like that.' He turned to the adults around him. 'I've read a legend about the Heart Eaters. It's just brilliant that the stories about them turn out to be true, and even more wonderful that one of their descendants is here, just when we need him most.'

Jonah felt a lot better but he still couldn't help feeling self-conscious with everyone's attention focused just on him. All this fuss was making him feel as if he was stealing the spotlight. After all, he was merely a visitor. The Last Great Dragon was a *Welsh* dragon. It ought to be Erin or one of her friends who had inherited the Heart Eater's power. Impulsively, he ran up to the gate.

'Do you want to help feed him?' he asked.

Gethin, with 'Wow, yes thanks. Great!' was over the gate immediately. Jonah nodded encouragingly at Erin. She blushed scarlet, and he could see she was scared and would have rather stayed on the other side of the wall, but she set her jaw and began to climb the gate. There was a roar from the lane and her father pushed his way through the crowd.

'Oh, no, you don't, my girl! Come back down here. It's not safe!'

'It is now, Dad. You heard Saint Michael. Jonah can control the dragon.' Erin, astride the field gate, was looking obstinate.

'Erin!' Her father bellowed, but she dropped into the field and turned to face him.

'It's OK, Daddy, really,' she said sweetly. 'It is safe, honestly.

And I won't go too near.'

Her father groaned. 'Duw, where does she get it from?' he asked nobody in particular and laughed reluctantly when someone shouted, 'From her Dad, Emlyn, isn't it?'

It was difficult pulling the freezer bags away from the frozen food. The plastic wrap stuck, and the children's fingers began to sting with the cold.

'Hey,' said Gethin. 'Wouldn't he be better at this?' And he nodded towards the dragon.

'Oh, yeah. Good thinking.' Jonah picked up a couple of the frozen packets and took them over to Ffyrnig. He told the dragon to breathe gently over the frozen meat and beamed with satisfaction when he was able to peel the wrappings away easily. 'There you go,' he said. 'Just blow on it until it's nice to eat.'

Ffyrnig sniffed at the pile of chops and pieces of chicken on the grass and looked disdainful. 'Why is it hard and cold?' he asked.

Jonah laughed. 'It's a way of keeping meat fresh till we need it,' he explained.

The dragon looked uncertain but blew carefully, and rumbled with pleasure as blood began to seep into the grass. He nosed at the pieces of meat and then started swallowing the portions eagerly. Gethin started forward with some more packages. As fast as the boys unwrapped them, the dragon gulped down the food. Gethin, pulling a joint from its plastic wrapper, turned round to find Ffyrnig's great horned head almost on his shoulder. Jumping hastily backwards, he tripped and the piece of beef flipped out of his grasp. Ffyrnig thrust his neck forward and caught it neatly, swallowing it whole. The children cheered and the watching crowd, beginning to lose their fear, started clapping and laughing. Ffyrnig, delighted by his audience, began showing off. He caught some linked sausages with his forefeet and, with a sweeping lunge that almost tore a hawthorn tree out of the hedge, twirled them round and round in the air before flinging them up and swallowing them. His audience yelled and laughed and clapped, until their hands were sore.

'That's it,' said Jonah. 'You've finished the starters, Ffyrnig. But there'll be a proper meal for you soon.'

Erin and Gethin were giggling again.

'What's the matter?' Jonah wanted to know.

'You. Gossiping away with a big lizard,' Gethin said.

Jonah grinned. 'OK, you talk to him then.'

'Tell him the next meat won't be frozen,' said Erin, but when Jonah did, she collapsed into giggles again.

'You're hopeless, you two,' he said good-naturedly, and turned to explain what the joke was to Ffyrnig.

The dragon squeezed his eyes nearly shut, which Jonah had begun to realise was his way of showing pleasure. 'They won't laugh when they see what you can do,' he said. 'Climb on my back and I'll take you for a ride. You'll be quite safe,' he added, as he noticed a hint of doubt in Jonah's eyes. 'My back isn't at all slippery, and you can sit on my shoulders between my wings and hold on.'

Jonah's face was eager but he was still slightly hesitant. He didn't want to look like a show-off.

'Come on, Master,' coaxed the dragon. 'I won't fly very high!'

Jonah bit his lip.

'You're a Dragoneer, Master. You ought to know how to ride on my back. What if the angels need help somewhere else?'

Jonah could not resist any longer. What Ffyrnig had just said made sense. He ran forward, stepped up on to Ffyrnig's thigh and pulled himself up on to the dragon's back. It was unexpectedly easy. He settled himself in the narrow space at the base of the dragon's huge wings and held on to the thick, tough edges, with his legs gripping Ffyrnig's spine. He was surprised how comfortable it was. The dragon's scales were warm and it was rather like sitting on a very, very large heated leather saddle.

'Ready?' asked Ffyrnig.

'Yes!' Jonah replied in a voice taut with excitement. He could hear cries of alarm from the churchyard as Claire and Bryn realised what was happening, but he tried to ignore them. *I know he'll look after me. It will be all right.*

'Hold tight!' The dragon turned towards the corner of the meadow on the far side from the lane, rose high on his legs, ran forward a few steps at enormous speed until he was almost on the other side of the field and then launched himself upwards into the air. A great yell burst out of Jonah's mouth. He held on tensely but soon realised Ffyrnig had been right. His back wasn't at all slippery. Jonah felt completely safe, gripped between the dragon's shoulder blades.

Ffyrnig flew lazily up the Cascob valley and out over the Radnor Forest. A warm wind blew Jonah's hair back and he could smell the not unpleasant smokiness of Ffyrnig's breath, as it streamed past him. Looking down, he could see the dragon's huge shadow passing over a green carpet of trees, and then they were out over hilly uplands.

Hanging on tightly, Jonah peered down at the sunlit meadows below them. Riding the dragon was more exciting, he thought, than even the best funfair ride. Better even than 'The Big One' at Blackpool Pleasure Beach. Ffyrnig dipped and swooped freely through the air, and Jonah wanted to shout aloud. As they began to glide back, down towards Cascob, he could not help feeling thrilled that Ffyrnig had woken up. In spite of the terrible things that the Night Creatures might do, now that they could escape from the Underworld, it was still exciting to be with a dragon.

I'm riding the Last Great Dragon of Wales, he thought, *and I am his Dragoneer. Wow!*

And he whooped, as they came gently down towards the meadow, and he saw all the upturned faces waiting for them.

Chapter 20

TROUBLE IN HEREFORD

An early supper was just finishing in the big old kitchen at Maesglas Farm. Claire had asked the Morgans and Rhodri to eat with them. In fact, Gwen had been at Maesglas all day, while Bryn and Emlyn, Rhodri and Ted had worked together on the jobs that had to be done on both farms. Jonah and Erin had spent most of the day with the dragon, and there was a constant stream of onlookers up and down the lane to watch Ffyrnig munching the huge pile of joints the Knighton butcher had brought for him. Nobody could settle down to an ordinary day. They wanted to talk about the Last Great Dragon and the demons, and exclaim about seeing real angels in the sky and how amazing it was to find out that Mike was really the Archangel Michael.

'*Please* come and eat with us,' Claire had said at the end of the long, hot afternoon. 'You'll be doing Jonah a kindness.' She rolled her eyes at him. 'It might just stop me hammering him to a pulp.'

'Oh, Claire! I've said I'm sorry. About a million times!'

'Yes,' said Bryn. 'Leave it alone now, love. He *has* said he's sorry you were worried. And, in any case, what boy his age could have said "no" to a ride on a dragon? Give me the chance and I'll have a go! *Ouch*.' He threw up his arms to cover his head as Claire, laughing, hit him with a cushion.

'Hopeless,' she said to Gwen. 'How can I stop Jonah riding the dragon, when all these chaps want a go on it, too? It's probably a good thing that we can't get a phone signal because I don't know what I'd say to Jonah's mum. My sister will be frantic when she hears that he's been riding around the sky on a creature that *she* thinks just exists in stories. She'll say I'm mad and, what's more, totally irresponsible as an aunt!'

Everyone was laughing when Rhodri held up a hand for quiet. 'Was that someone knocking just now?'

'Yes, it was,' said a voice and Mike Golding walked into the kitchen. At least, he looked like Mike Golding but, of course, they all knew who he really was. Everyone stopped talking and Emlyn Morgan stood up and pulled out a chair for him.

'Thanks,' said the angel. He looked round at all the respectful faces and began to grin. 'Please, everybody, try to forget you have seen me with wings! Just treat me like you did before. Yes?'

'That's, like, impossible. No one could forget how big your wings are. And when you have them, it's hard to look straight at you, too. Did you know that you glow?'

'Erin!' Gwen shushed her fiercely.

Mike laughed. 'No, Gwen. Erin is right. I know I'm asking a lot, but I would like it very much if you all just treated me as a friend. However,' Mike turned to Jonah, 'I do come as an angelic messenger, I'm afraid. Something terrible is happening in Hereford.'

'What's that?' Rhodri asked.

It seemed that the Night Creatures were beginning to swarm into Hereford. They had appeared suddenly in the morning, descending on the cathedral, and more were arriving, getting bolder all the time. They were leaping about on the cathedral roof and scurrying around Cathedral Green. The creatures had even gone as far as the beginning of Capuchin Lane, the little alley that led to High Town, where they were terrifying those shopkeepers who lived on the premises.

'The police have closed the roads into the centre of Hereford,' said Mike, 'and they are stopping people from walking into the area round the cathedral. When the first gargoyles started hopping about on the roof, lots of passers-by stopped to stare, and the creatures loved that!'

Jonah and Erin both started to speak.

'Did many come down on the ground?'

'Did anyone get hurt?'

'Quite a few, yes,' Mike replied to Jonah. Then he turned to Erin. 'I'm afraid some people have been injured. Of course, nobody could understand what sort of creatures they were looking at. Two of the cathedral staff went to investigate and were mauled, and a policeman who went to help them was seriously wounded. Other onlookers soon realised they had to keep well away. The clergy still don't know exactly what they are dealing with, so there could be more accidents. The bishop needs to know that we can help.'

'What I can't understand,' said Bryn, 'is why demons should *want* to be on the cathedral. You'd think that was the last place they would go.'

Mike nodded. 'Well, the thing is, they want to keep you away from it. They don't want human beings to gain strength by going to church together. And don't forget that they might inhabit the Underworld now, but they lived in Heaven once, before they fell from grace. They are mad with longing for what they have lost.'

'I suppose,' said Claire, 'the churches we've built seem like a kind of paradise to them. So, although the cathedral frightens them, they'd still like to turn us out and take it for themselves.'

'What you might call a love/hate relationship,' Erin commented brightly.

Mike's lips twitched as he looked at her.

'You might well say that,' he replied drily. 'And, of course, the cathedral is where the gargoyles are. The demons enter them to use their shapes, and then they cling together, getting used to the atmosphere of Upper Earth, I suppose. Then, when they are ready, I'm afraid they will start coming down en masse to attack people.'

Claire was looking puzzled. 'Mike, you said there were swarms of the things. There aren't enough gargoyles on the cathedral for them all, are there?'

Mike shook his head. 'No, but we all know that one evil begets another. Some demons don't need a stone gargoyle to inhabit. That kind seem to have more power and are able to assume an earthly body at will. They just copy the look.'

Erin made a face. 'The demon as fashion victim!' she murmured to Jonah. Her father shook his head at her, warningly.

'The gremlins have completely messed up the telephone and radio systems, so the whole area is cut off from the rest of Britain. Nobody knows what's going on and there's growing panic. I'm afraid that before we can stop it, armed police will be brought in. The Night Creatures won't be injured, of course, but they *will* get really maddened. That will make a bad situation worse.'

Erin looked puzzled. 'Mike, why aren't the angels getting rid of them like they did this morning?'

'Well,' said Mike, 'I've left the others trying to drive them back into the Abyss but, like I told you, we can only fight them one at a time. That will take ages and, even then, it would be quite possible for some of them to hide from us.'

There was silence in the kitchen for a moment, and then Mike patted Jonah's shoulder and turned to Claire. 'Ffyrnig's fire power is so intense, he could sweep hundreds of gremlins away with just one or two passes over the cathedral, leaving the angels free to turn them out of the lanes and search out any hiding places. But we need Jonah to tell him what to do.'

Claire drew in her breath and Bryn put a steadying hand on her arm.

Mike nodded gravely. 'Yes, I'm sorry, Claire, but we can't do without the help of the Great Dragon and that means Jonah too.'

'Yes, I see,' said Claire reluctantly. 'But it'll be so dangerous for Jonah if the police start shooting!' She shook her head. 'No. I'm sorry but I really can't allow this!'

'Claire!' Jonah reddening with anger, shoved back his chair. 'You can't say that! How can Ffyrnig manage, if I don't go?'

'And how can I tell your parents, if you get shot?'

Rhodri pushed back his chair and stood up. 'We can make

sure that doesn't happen. I'll go down to Credenhill and explain everything to one of the officers. If they speak with the police and help take charge—'

'But the SAS will never believe you,' Emlyn objected. 'They'll think you've gone off your rocker.'

'Not if I go with him,' said Mike. 'I will show them who I am.'

They all exchanged looks, imagining the scene at the Credenhill barracks, as Mike revealed his real self.

'Brilliant!' exclaimed Jonah, after a moment. 'And I've just thought of something else. If the Vicar of Knighton went to the cathedral, he could explain everything to the bishop, couldn't he? Until you could get there, I mean.'

Mike thought this was a good idea. 'It's best for everyone at the cathedral and the police station to be prepared for the dragon, before you actually arrive. Otherwise, he'll cause such a commotion, that the Night Creatures will be able to get among the crowd and fan out into the city streets.'

Claire gave Jonah an apologetic smile. 'I don't mean to treat you like a little kid, you know.'

'I do know,' he said quietly. And then he grinned. 'You wouldn't be much of an aunt if you said, "Well, you might get shot, but don't let it bother you," would you?'

Emlyn said he would drive to Knighton and speak to the vicar. 'And if he's not there, I'll find another clergyman who was at Cascob this morning,' he said.

'Shall we go with Dad?' Gwen asked Erin.

Jonah looked across at Erin. She was nodding at her mother but Jonah felt awkward. Here he was, the centre of attention again, going to help fight the demons, while Erin would have to learn what happened from other people. It didn't seem fair. After all, it was Erin who had taken him to Cascob and told him all about the Last Great Dragon of Wales. He touched Gwen's arm.

'Please,' he said, 'I really need Erin to come with me.'

Erin turned with wide eyes. A huge smile lit her face, as she realised what Jonah meant.

'On Ffyrnig? Oh, yesss!' She danced up and down.

Emlyn was horrified. 'Oh, look, Jonah. Wait a minute here...'

Jonah rushed in before anyone could come up with reasons why Erin shouldn't go. 'She has such good ideas and – er – she knows Hereford. I've never even been there. Erin could make sure that I'm right when I tell Ffyrnig where to go and what to do.' He looked round at all the anxious faces. '*Please*. I need her.'

'Best if you take a grown-up,' Rhodri said.

Jonah bit his lip. He hadn't thought of that.

Bryn stroked his chin. 'Might that be a bit of a burden for the dragon, if he's having to manoeuvre round rooftops?'

'Well, he's so big that it would probably be OK,' Rhodri said. 'but we'd better be on the safe side. Perhaps it *would* be a good idea if Erin went with Jonah.'

There was complete silence for a moment and then Gwen spoke. 'We should let her go, Emlyn. Jonah's only the same age as she is, and if he can do this for people, well – we shouldn't stop Erin from helping him.' She waited for Emlyn's answer.

He looked hard at both children and then, while Erin and Jonah waited, hardly daring to breathe, he leaned forward and cupped Erin's face. 'You go with Jonah, *cariad*. And mind you're both very careful.' And he smiled at them.

Erin threw her arms round him. 'Thanks, Daddy. We'll be careful – and sensible. I promise. Won't we, Jonah?'

Solemnly, he nodded at Emlyn. 'We won't take risks,' he said.

Chapter 21

HELP FROM CREDENHILL

Jonah was in the meadow with Ffyrnig, telling him how they had been asked to help exterminate the Night Creatures in Hereford. The sun was low in the sky, throwing long shadows on the grass, when he heard the roar of vehicles in the lane.

'I think Rhodri and Mike are back,' he said to the dragon. 'Hang on. I'll just go and see. Are you ready, if they want us to go now?' He stopped and thought. 'Can you see OK in the dark? I mean, it could be late by the time we've caught all the Night Creatures.'

The great dragon rumbled with laughter.

'OK. Silly question,' Jonah said good-naturedly, remembering how much time dragons were said to spend underground. 'I'll just go and see if we're really going.'

As he started towards the field gate, Rhodri and Mike came into the meadow with three men who were wearing motorcycle leathers.

'You're on, Jonah,' said Rhodri. He turned to the three strangers, who were staring at Ffyrnig. Jonah noticed that, unlike everyone else on first seeing the dragon, they did not look frightened of him, just intensely interested.

'This is our Dragoneer, Jonah Drake,' Rhodri said. 'Jonah, these gentlemen are former colleagues of mine from Credenhill barracks. This is... '

One of the men flashed a glance at Rhodri, who checked himself and went on, 'Er... Sam, Henry and Ollie.' They shook hands and the tall man called Sam, who seemed to be the leader, smiled at Jonah.

'So you only learned this afternoon that you're a – erm –

Dragoneer,' he said.

'Yes. It was a bit of a shock.'

Sam grinned and nodded, then he looked over at Ffyrnig, who was eyeing them lazily. 'I'd like to see you in operation, Jonah. Could I watch you getting the dragon to do something – get him to his feet or something like that?' He turned to Mike. 'I need to watch this young man's interaction with the dragon, Sir, so that I can assess safety issues if it does go to Hereford.' He glanced over at Ffyrnig. 'There's a lot of firepower sitting there. If anything goes wrong, it could be disastrous.'

Mike smiled. 'I understand that. But you'll find Jonah has complete control.'

'I could ask him to fly up the valley for you,' Jonah said shyly.

'Excellent. Thank you,' said Sam.

Jonah felt as if he had stepped into the pages of an adventure story. Incredibly, he was going to show SAS soldiers something that they had never done themselves. He ran over to Ffyrnig. 'Those men are soldiers from a very special regiment. They want to see us fly up the valley.'

'Us?' queried Ffyrnig, lowering his eyelids. 'From the way they behaved, I got the impression that they are only expecting to watch me.'

'Well, maybe. But they want to see how we get on together and they won't, will they, if I don't come, too?' He could not wait to be on Ffyrnig's back again and, as he admitted to himself, it was even more of a thrill to ride the dragon with SAS troopers watching.

The men were busy chatting. Right.

'Could you help me on, please, Ffyrnig.' He scrambled up the dragon's lowered wing and settled himself comfortably between Ffyrnig's shoulder blades. He heard surprised shouts, saw Mike and Rhodri beginning to laugh, and then Ffyrnig had swung towards the far corner of the meadow and was pounding across the grass for take-off. They rushed upwards, and the hilltops slid away below Ffyrnig's vast wings. Jonah's hair blew back as Ffyrnig raced westward towards the flame-coloured sky, where the sun was dipping below the horizon. Jonah tugged on Ffyrnig's wing.

'We'll go back now. When you turn, can you breathe out some fire?' he called. 'Show them what you can do.'

'I will, Master,' Ffyrnig agreed, and as they sped back towards Cascob, a great spurt of fire poured into the air above the valley. Jonah could just hear the exclamations of the figures in the field, as the dragon glided carefully down and tucked his great length into the meadow once again.

The men beamed as they came up to Ffyrnig and Jonah. Sam slapped him on the back.

'That was quite something,' he said. 'The power of the animal! Riding it must be amazing.'

'He certainly thinks it is,' Rhodri laughed, nodding towards Jonah.

The soldiers and Ffyrnig gazed intently at each other.

'Magnificent,' Henry murmured.

Jonah beamed at Ffyrnig. 'Henry thinks you're magnificent.'

Ffyrnig was pleased. 'Discerning fellow,' he purred in a smoky voice, startling the soldiers, who jumped back and then began to laugh.

Ollie was rubbing his chin thoughtfully. 'The dragon seemed to react when you made those reptile noises to it.' He was too polite to suggest that it was weird to chat with a dragon. Mike and Jonah grinned.

'Jonah was born with the ability to communicate with dragons,' Mike said.

Sam stared. 'Communicate—'

'But it feels just as if we're speaking English,' Jonah explained. 'I don't know how it works. It just does.'

The soldiers shook their heads in surprise.

Sam studied Ffyrnig thoughtfully for a moment and then

turned to Mike. 'You can guarantee, Sir, that the dragon cannot be killed by modern weapons?'

'I'm absolutely sure,' Mike confirmed. 'But we need to protect the children, in case anybody tries.'

'And we'll need to get that information out into the city. We'll mount a loudspeaker on a truck to tour the streets round the centre,' said Sam. 'Ollie, would you get back to the barracks and organise that, please.'

An Army vehicle was bringing some helmets and protective clothing to the farm for Erin and Jonah to try on, and Sam had also ordered some webbing harness and netting.

'We'll fashion some kind of a netting cage to secure around the dragon's wings,' he said, 'to stop you sliding off his back.'

'Ffyrnig isn't slippery,' Jonah began to object but he saw Mike raise an eyebrow. 'Well, I suppose it would be safer for us if Ffyrnig has to swerve about a lot,' he admitted.

'And you can't both tuck in between Ffyrnig's shoulders,' added Mike. He smiled at Jonah. 'I must go. Sam will get you and Erin kitted out and harnessed safely on Ffyrnig's back. By now, the SAS will have told the police that firearms are useless against the Night Creatures and people will be panicking. It's time that we went to Hereford, Jonah. Come as soon as you can.'

The air around Mike shivered and brightened. His form seemed to waver in an orb of brilliant golden light. They saw the indistinct outline of great, feathered wings and had a glimpse of golden curls blowing back from his uplifted face, and then Saint Michael had gone.

The trooper named Henry whistled. 'Wow!' he breathed to the others. 'I never thought I'd see a sight like that.'

'Right. Come on then, Jonah,' said Rhodri, squeezing his shoulder. 'Let's get you two kitted out. It's time for our Last Great Dragon to show what he can do.'

Chapter 22

FLYING TO BATTLE

Jonah, with Erin tucked in behind him, was sitting in the webbing cage fixed on Ffyrnig's red-bronze back. They both felt strange and awkward in their helmets, boots and protective suits; it was as if they were dressed for parts in a film.

'I can't believe this is happening,' Erin said. 'Do you think it's going to be dangerous?'

'It is for the demons! You're not afraid, are you?'

'A bit,' she admitted. 'Jonah?'

'What?'

She rushed the words out. 'Thanks for getting Mam and Dad to let me come with you. It's really nice of you.'

Jonah was embarrassed. 'It's OK,' he said gruffly. 'It wasn't fair for me to have all the interesting stuff. I didn't choose my ancestors.'

He heard her whisper 'Thanks,' and then Sam was signalling from the field gate. Rhodri and the two soldiers were on their motorbikes ready to ride down to Hereford. Jonah waved back.

'Right, Ffyrnig. Time to go. Down the valley.' Then the dragon turned and pounded over the field, pulled up his legs with a roar and leaped into the air. They soared into the darkening sky with a speed that took their breath away. Erin gasped and clutched Jonah's back. The sun was now a red glow over to their right.

'Are we going the right way?' yelled Jonah.

Erin gazed down. 'Yes, look, see those lights on the right? That's Kington. Dad said we just keep the sunset a bit behind us, on our right as well, and go in a straight line from there, and that will take us to Hereford.'

The shadowy countryside raced below the dragon's huge

wings as Ffyrnig flew high and silently over Herefordshire. Jonah imagined that very few people would notice the dragon soaring above their homes.

'You can hear planes and you see their lights winking but there's nothing to draw attention to Ffyrnig,' he said. 'I bet he could fly around after dark, high in the sky, and nobody would be any the wiser.'

He could feel the little gold locket that Claire had given him while he was putting on his safety gear, on a chain round his neck.

'Oh, no,' he had protested. 'Not a necklace, Claire.'

'No one will know you're wearing it,' she coaxed, 'but your mum gave it to me on my twenty-first birthday. So I've put the *Abracadabra* charm inside to protect you.'

'I've already got one. It's in my jeans pocket. Look.'

'Yes, but I'd like you to have this as well. As if your mum is watching over you.'

'Well, all right then,' he had mumbled. 'Thanks. I'll put it in my pocket.'

'Where it can easily fall out! Put it round your neck, Jonah. Please.'

He had been going to argue but then he saw that her lower lip was trembling.

'I have to try to keep you safe,' she had said, 'for your mum and dad.'

So he had hugged her, and now the feel of the little locket against his skin was comforting.

Erin shook his shoulder. 'Look. See the really dark sprawl ahead of us? We're nearly there.'

Jonah thumped Ffyrnig's back to get the dragon's attention and asked him to fly lower, so that they would know when they got near the centre of the city. Ffyrnig dropped height as they passed over clustered roofs that showed they were on the outskirts. Erin tapped Jonah's shoulder.

'Look, that's Credenhill down there. See the barracks? Oh, and just look!'

As they peered down at the SAS lines, they could see small figures below them, waving.

'Wow!' breathed Jonah. 'They were looking out for us.'

'I know!' Erin wriggled excitedly.

'Steady on,' grumbled Ffyrnig. 'Tell her that tickles.'

In a few moments, the dragon was circling the city centre. Staring down, Jonah and Erin began to feel apprehensive. Jonah had imagined that the streets would be empty but throngs of people were milling around in a wide space, not far from where he could see the bulk of the cathedral.

'That's High Town,' Erin said, 'where the main shops are.'

As the Great Dragon loomed over the crowd, people began screaming and scrambled for cover. Jonah looked down anxiously. How could Ffyrnig burn out the gremlins, if there were crowds all around? The dragon's fire would cause terrible injuries, if anyone got in the way.

'I thought Mike said the police had blocked the roads,' he yelled over his shoulder. He peered down at some people who huddled in terror against the front of Marks and Spencer, trying to hide away from the dragon. He wished he could let them know that Ffyrnig wouldn't hurt them. As they passed over the shop's roof, he was relieved to see policemen manning a barrier across a narrow lane.

'Here we are,' Erin said. 'This leads to Cathedral Green.'

'This is it,' Jonah called to the dragon.

Erin clutched Jonah's arm. 'It's all seemed like a dream till now but this is really happening, isn't it?' She drew in a deep breath. 'Jonah, if anything bad happens—'

'It won't. We'll be OK.' Jonah sounded a lot more confident than he felt.

'Yes, I know. I'm sure we will. But I just wanted to say, like, I wouldn't want *not* to be here, even if it did go all wrong.'

'Me too,' Jonah said.

Ffyrnig circled just above the rooftops. Leaning over to look down, the children could see that all the roads leading to Hereford Cathedral were blocked off, and there were policemen and soldiers around the edge of the close. There were crowds of people in the streets beyond the roadblocks and others hanging out of windows, all looking up in wonder at the unbelievable sight of a gigantic dragon circling their city in the still summer night. In the dim light, the huge cathedral roof looked strange. It seemed to be wavering. Jonah peered down until his eyes adjusted to what he was looking at.

There were Night Creatures, hundreds of them, all over the roof. They were crouching on the tiles, dangling from the pinnacles. Little yellow pinpricks, some tiny slits, some round like marbles, shone in the dark, showing that the demons' eyes were fixed on the dragon. The children became aware of an angry sound, like the loud hum of wasps. Then they saw small fiends in the trees surrounding the cathedral as well and, as Ffyrnig passed over the Green again, Jonah noticed some of the little beasts leaping down from the building on to the grass.

'Erin, look!' he turned and shouted. 'They're getting ready to attack. They'll be all over the policemen if we aren't quick.'

Erin looked around anxiously. 'I can't see the angels, Jonah. What will we do if they're not here? If the gremlins get away from Ffyrnig, we'll lose them in the alleys. They'll get into buildings.' Her voice rose with tension. 'People are going to die.'

'We are here, Erin,' called Michael's voice and the children swung round to see the Archangel flying upwards to drift beside them. He pointed to where, in the darkness beyond the cathedral, there seemed to be an open space with another large building silhouetted against it. 'That's the bishop's palace. We have been conferring with him in the courtyard.'

The dark area of the courtyard started to glimmer and angelic forms took shape and flew towards Cathedral Green. Ffyrnig beat his great wings slowly and hovered over the palace, as the angels rose into the air. The children heard a sound, like one enormous sigh, come from the crowded streets beyond the barriers. Saint Michael soared up and hovered by Ffyrnig's head, his robes glimmering in the summer darkness. 'Are you all ready? Start with the roof, Jonah. Let Ffyrnig destroy all the gremlins up there, before you start on the walls, and the nooks and crannies. We angels will guard the Cathedral Close and try to see that none of the creatures gets past us.'

Jonah swallowed and tried to speak calmly. 'Yes, we're ready, aren't we, Ffyrnig? You heard what Saint Michael wants you to do?'

The dragon rumbled; yes, he understood. Saint Michael smiled at them, as his golden-white wings beat the air. 'God bless you tonight,' he said. 'The other angels are in place now. Hold on tight to the netting and keep a tight watch.' And he swooped away to where Capuchin Lane ran into the Cathedral Green.

The dragon rumbled again.

'What's Ffyrnig saying?'

'That all we have to do is watch for Night Creatures. The rest is up to him. And he won't let us fall,' said Jonah. Then to Ffyrnig, 'OK. Let's go.'

Chapter 23

FIREPOWER

The dragon shot away from the city centre and then turned in a wide arc over the hills to the north.

'What's he doing?' yelled Erin in alarm.

'Ffyrnig!' Jonah shouted. 'Where are you going?'

'I have to have a long enough flight to power up my flames,' said Ffyrnig. 'Right. This should do it.'

Drawing his great, taloned limbs up tightly beneath his body, the dragon hovered for a moment. He gulped in huge draughts of air as he stoked up his inner fire. Jonah could feel Ffyrnig's leathery skin beginning to get warmer. Then, with a sudden screeching roar that made the children jump in their harnesses, Ffyrnig hurled himself towards the city. The rushing air tore screams out of their throats. Jonah felt Erin clutching his waist. Ffyrnig banked just before the cathedral, almost coming to a halt in the sky. His massive wings beat hard as he drew in a mighty breath. He shrieked and dived at the roof, aiming a massive jet of fire at the gargoyles. Hovering just above the cathedral, he swung his head from side to side, driving flames across the writhing mass of hideous little bodies.

Some fell lifeless instantaneously and lay like broken ornaments. Others threw themselves over the edge of the great roof, clinging to the guttering and gibbering. The choking fumes made the children cough, and they had to blink back tears. As the dragon passed and re-passed over the roof, emitting jets of flame, the Night Creatures screeched in fury as they scrabbled to get away.

Erin tugged urgently on Jonah's sleeve. 'Get Ffyrnig away from the roof, Jonah! Now!' She was screaming.

Jonah swivelled round. 'Why? What's the matter?'

'Look at the way they are sliding and skidding about. I think Ffyrnig is melting the roof! The leads look red-hot. The cathedral could burn down. Get him away!'

'Ffyrnig!' Jonah yelled. 'They're running on to the grass. Let's do the Cathedral Green now.'

The dragon swept over the trees, raking the lawns with flame. The scorched grass was covered with broken bodies as the demons left them and fled, vanishing into the night to find their way back to the Abyss. In Capuchin Lane and at the barriers, angels were swooping on gargoyles that had escaped Ffyrnig's fire. Golden swords flashed through the dark, as the angels dispatched the creatures. The children saw Saint Michael swing his sword down on a gargoyle's neck, severing head from body. Erin yelped as the grotesque head bounced into Capuchin Lane.

Jonah hammered on Ffyrnig's shoulder. 'That was great!' he coughed. 'Let's go back to finish off the roof.'

Ffyrnig hovered over the cathedral nave, beating his wings slowly as he peered down to look for any movement. The roof was strewn with bits of the broken stone images the Night Creatures had used. It looked as if the demons had all fled.

'I think we have finished here, Master,' the dragon boomed. 'And, in any case, I can't hover for much longer.'

'Why? What's wrong?'

Ffyrnig's wings were beating more slowly and the children could feel him taking great gasping breaths.

'At this height there isn't enough volume of air to hold me up. I am too big.'

Jonah patted Ffyrnig's shoulder. 'Oh, I see. Go on, then.'

Ffyrnig rose higher and they wheeled slowly around the city centre. Jonah looked down. Below them, two angels shone out of the darkness as they floated above the courtyard of the bishop's palace. He saw one raise his sword and heard a demon howl.

As the dragon turned, Jonah glanced to his right up the road that ran in front of the cathedral. Out of the corner of his eye, he caught a movement at the end of Broad Street, beyond the press of people at the barriers. A tall figure in a long robe was crossing the road. It was the whisperer in Jonah's nightmare visions; he was sure of it. The figure turned its hooded head towards the cathedral and, just for a second, Jonah got the impression that there was just blackness where its face should be. He shuddered, and then it had gone. As his eyes adjusted to the thicker darkness away from Cathedral Green, he noticed dark shapes speeding along the road.

'Erin! Look down there! Wolves. There are the wolves!'

'Where?' she yelled, leaning out over the webbing cage. 'Oh, no! They'll go for all those people!'

Helplessly, the children stared down as the wolves raced down Broad Street. People at the back of the crowd turned as they heard running feet and then the wolves were upon them. There was pandemonium as people fell beneath the creatures' weight or tried to break away. Jonah grasped Erin's arm.

'That's weird,' he shouted. 'Look. They're not actually attacking.'

'Totally weird. They are just pushing through.'

Jonah screwed up his eyes to gaze down. He watched as the biggest wolf knocked a policeman down and realised Erin was right. The creature took no notice of the man but just scrabbled over his body and leaped across the barrier, while screaming people scattered, and let the rest of the pack through. The wolves streamed on to Cathedral Green and then milled about, running up and down, rooting about among the gargoyle bodies. As Ffyrnig wheeled over the cathedral again, the pack leader raised its muzzle and howled. All the people who had been crowded at the barriers were retreating down the three roads that met at the Green, and the children, looking down, saw heads turn in alarm at the mournful wail.

'What's up with it?' Jonah said.

'I think it didn't find what it was looking for.' Erin sounded scared.

Jonah, puzzled, turned towards her.

'What do you think it *was* looking for?'

'You,' she said, in a tiny voice.

Chapter 24

THE DEMON ON THE ROOF

Jonah turned in his harness and stared at Erin. She gazed at him anxiously from under her helmet.

'I think you've been the target all along.'

'But – but why?'

'I don't know. It's just, like, a feeling I have.' She bit her lip.

The wolf pack had moved past the cathedral's north door and disappeared in the darkness at the other end of the great building. Some of the crowd were running back up Broad Street, but Jonah saw that others had pushed the barrier over and clambered over it, venturing cautiously on to Cathedral Green.

'Oh, the idiots! Don't they realise how dangerous it is?'

Erin pointed down towards the east end of the main cathedral building where a couple of wolves were casting about, sniffing the ground, and looking around in search of something.

'Jonah, do something!' she gasped. 'There are too many people round the cathedral now. When those wolves don't find you – if it is you they're looking for – they'll get angry, and then they *might* start killing people.'

He stared round at her in desperation. They both guessed that dragon fire might destroy people as well as the demon wolves.

'Ffyrnig, we've got to find Saint Michael,' Jonah shouted urgently. The dragon swung away towards the bishop's palace, passing carefully over the cathedral while the children anxiously searched for the Archangel. Ffyrnig flew as low and as slowly as he dared, close to the pinnacles that decorated the cathedral roofs. Jonah felt a tug on the webbing as Erin twisted to look round and then, without warning, a big, grey, leathery arm shot out from behind one of the ornamental pinnacles and yanked her out of the webbing cage.

Next moment, Erin was dangling in the air, shrieking with terror. A huge gargoyle was gripping one of her arms, while her body was still attached to Ffyrnig by the safety harness. Horrified, Jonah saw that, with all the noise and confusion below them, the dragon hadn't realised who was screaming. If he flew on, Erin would be ripped out of the harness, and either savaged or dropped to her death.

'Stop, Ffyrnig. Stop. It's got Erin!' He was thumping on the dragon's back, yelling to him to stop moving. Ffyrnig swung his head round, saw Erin hanging from the demon's claws and drew in a great breath. Gingerly, he edged nearer to the roof of the nave, beating his wings as slowly as he could, so that he could hover there.

'Master,' he panted, 'tell her to keep still. If she fights, the creature might drop her.'

'Erin, don't fight. Don't fight.' Panic made Jonah's voice sound high and squeaky.

The Night Creature, which looked like a deformed, horned ape with wings, chuckled as it swung Erin backwards and forwards. It dropped her down suddenly, pretending to let go, and then yanked her upwards again. Even in the dark, Jonah could see that she was white with terror. He twisted round, desperately searching for Saint Michael and then jumped with shock as Ffyrnig sent a great jet of fire down to the ground.

'What are you doing?' Jonah yelled.

'Hot air helps me hover for longer.'

Turning back to Erin, he saw the gargoyle ape was starting to pull her on to the roof.

She'll be torn in two! Jonah saw at once what he had to do. He took a deep breath and fought down the panic that was making him shake. He reached over and began to free Erin's harness from the netting. His fingers felt like clumsy sausages as he struggled frantically with the buckle. At last it was undone. Even if the gargoyle dragged her away or, worse still, threw her over the parapet, at least she wouldn't be ripped apart.

The creature had both its skinny claws round her arm, and was dragging her up and over the guttering. She grabbed at the parapet with her free hand and the demon, face contorted in fury, jumped on her and savagely bit her neck. Erin screamed with pain. The demon began to pull her up the scorching leaded roof. Jonah knew he had to do something fast. Ffyrnig couldn't help; if he burned the demon, he would burn Erin too. And they could not wait for the Archangel. Jonah gritted his teeth and began to unbuckle his own harness.

'I've got to get on the roof, Ffyrnig! Can you go closer?'

Cautiously, he stood up, holding on to the webbing cage. The dragon beat the air with slow, massive strokes. Jonah stepped out of the cage and crouched down, out of the way of the dragon's wings. He edged carefully down Ffyrnig's back until he thought it was safe to stand up again. Then he straightened, balancing with outstretched arms. He could tell that Ffyrnig was straining every muscle in a huge effort to keep in one place without jolting him off. Even so, standing on the dragon's back felt like riding a skateboard with particularly loose wheels. He dared not look down, in case he felt giddy and fell. He fixed his eyes on the guttering, took a deep breath and jumped. He clawed at the hot stonework of the parapet, and hung on, legs frantically scrabbling for a foothold. Gasping with relief, the dragon shot away and soared upwards.

The gargoyle screeched and laughed. It had pulled Erin up to the top of the roof, where she lay like a rag doll on the hot shingles. The creature shook its fists at Jonah, glaring first at him and then back at Erin. It seemed to be wondering whether she could escape. Dare it leave her in order to rush at the boy? For the moment, it looked from one to the other, grimacing vilely, while Jonah heaved himself up and over the parapet on to the leads. They were unbearably hot.

He pulled himself upright against a pinnacle and leaned against it, hopping from one foot to the other. Thank goodness Claire had made him take the *Abracadabra* charm. Leaning against the stonework for support, he fumbled inside his shirt to make sure it was there, while the demon leered and snarled, making little mock runs towards him, and then turning back to crouch over Erin. Any minute now, Jonah knew, it would leave her to attack him.

He began to haul himself up the leads. His legs felt shaky and the lead strips burned his hands so that he had to keep snatching them up. His heart thundered in his chest, but he willed himself to crawl towards the demon. *Don't look down,* he told himself. *You can do it. You've got to. You've got to.*

The gargoyle was prancing around, squawking with glee. With a mighty heave, Jonah pushed himself to his feet and struggled crabwise up the roof towards it. The creature yelled, its face alight with cruelty, and leaped at him, grabbing his shoulders and clinging to his waist with its hind feet. He staggered under its weight and it laughed into his face, almost nose to nose. Jonah pulled violently away, gagging at its stinking breath, and fell backwards.

He felt himself beginning to slide down the roof with the beast on top of him. Its bony fingers dug into his flesh, and its legs gripped his waist with all its might. Jonah turned his head away from the gargoyle's foul stench and felt its saliva dripping on his cheek. As they bumped downwards, with Jonah's head and back scraping painfully on the edges of the leads, he fought to brace his heels and stop the slide. His fingers scrabbled for a hold and found the edge of a burning-hot tile. Summoning all his strength, Jonah held on with one hand while he felt for the locket. He clung on desperately, wincing at the pain in his hand, while the gargoyle's horny fingers dug into him. The demon leaned away chortling, opened its mouth wide to show yellowing fangs and lunged forward to bite. Jonah rammed the little pendant against its cheekbone, shouting the spell aloud. 'Abracadabra, abracadabra...'

The demon shrieked and rolled off his body, holding its head. Its eyes blazed with malice as it stared at Jonah. Gripping the locket tightly with his right hand, Jonah intoned, 'O Lord, grant that this holy charm ABRACADABRA may cure thy servants Erin Morgan and Jonah Drake from all evil spirits and from all their diseases. Amen.'

The demon, holding its face as if it hurt, chattered with anger but it retreated as Jonah inched towards it with the locket held out. He fixed his eyes on the creature as it crouched on the lead strips, glaring at him. Then, with a howl, it sprang at him again. Jonah fell sideways with the demon astride him. He heard a tinkling sound as the chain of Claire's locket snapped. The pendant skidded down towards the gutter. The Night Creature cackled with mirth as its bony fingers tightened round his arm. Jonah felt a rush of fury.

'What do you want?' he screamed.

The demon opened its mouth. Out of its throat came a dreadful, echoing voice, like something moaning in a hollow cavern. 'We want our home back. Our beautiful Earth. You must die, puny humans, and leave the land to us.'

'No! Never! It's not yours to take,' Jonah yelled. 'Get away. Saint Michael protects us. *Saint Michael protects us.*'

He brought his elbow up and rammed it into the gargoyle. The shock made the creature loosen its grip for a second and gave Jonah the chance to roll away, but the movement made him lose his hold. He shrieked as he felt himself sliding, hurtling down the hot leads towards the low stone parapet. As he slid, his body gathered momentum. There was nothing he could grab to slow his speed. The back of his head banged on the scorching shingles. Then his feet struck the parapet with a terrible jolt and a searing pain shot through his legs. The impact bounced him up and over the edge. A scream ripped from his throat, as the ground flew towards him.

Chapter 25

TO THE ABYSS

As Jonah was hurled towards the ground, a screeching cry rang round the Cathedral Green. He felt himself jerked upwards, held by sharp spikes which dug into his sides and made him groan aloud. The air whistled past his ears. He hung upside down from Ffyrnig's claws, looking up at the dragon's massive red belly. Hereford's streets waltzed giddily below them, until Jonah began to feel sick.

The dragon turned and glided back over the cathedral, hardly beating his wings. As they came to the Vicars' cloisters, he flew very low. Jonah could see his head turning from side to side.

'I am looking for somewhere safe to put you down, Master,' he said, 'I think this should do. There don't seem to be any Night Creatures left on this side of the precinct.' He landed carefully in the darkened quadrangle and placed Jonah on the grass.

'Did I hurt you much?' Ffyrnig's forehead was screwed up with concern. 'I can only pick things up by digging my claws in tight.'

'No,' Jonah lied, panting, and hoping that a small untruth to save Ffyrnig's feelings wouldn't count as lying to him. 'Thanks for catching me. That was brill.' He stared up at the dragon's anxious face. 'What about Erin, though? That ape thing might have killed her! Ffyrnig, see if you can get to her. And please hurry.'

'I'm going. I can't take off here, though. Not enough space. I'll have to go outside.' He nudged Jonah with his nose. 'I'm pretty sure the angels emptied this quadrangle of demons but be careful, won't you, Master?'

Jonah patted his leg. 'Yes. 'Course. But go on, Ffyrnig, please.'

He lay on the grass for a while, breathing heavily and gingerly stretching his legs and arms. There was just enough moonlight for him to be able to examine his sides. He undid his protective jacket. It had ridden up under his arms as he slid down the roof, so Ffyrnig's claws had ripped his tee-shirt. There were some bleeding scratches and sore red patches on his skin, but it could have been worse. He guessed he would have some huge bruises from falling down the roof, though. He fastened the jacket again and cautiously got to his feet. He felt in his jeans pockets for the paper with the spell. It was still there. Carefully, he put it in one of the zipped jacket pockets, so that it wouldn't easily drop out. He felt sad about Claire's pendant. Maybe someone would find it, though. He would tell Saint Michael and one of the cathedral staff how he had lost it on the roof.

He looked all round the cloisters. A couple of doorways, opening from the cathedral into the arcaded corridors, sent fingers of light across the grass, but it was too dark to see much. Jonah unzipped his pocket again and fingered the charm paper nervously. He prayed that the angels really had cleared the demons from the area. He kept looking over his shoulder. At any moment he expected a triumphant screech, as a gargoyle came racing towards him.

His body ached all over but, even though it hurt, he could walk. He felt exposed in the middle of the quadrangle so, as quietly as he could, he hobbled to an entrance into the cloister and pressed close against a pillar. Here, it would be harder for anyone – or *anything* – to make him out in the shadows, and he would be able to call to Ffyrnig when the dragon came back.

Oh, please, let Erin be all right. If the demon had killed her, it would all be down to him. Her parents would never have let her come to fight the Night Creatures, if he hadn't begged them. Miserably, Jonah wrapped his arms round his aching body, holding himself together.

As he stood there, desperately hoping for Ffyrnig to return, there was a slight sound at the other end of the corridor. Jonah swung round. He stared at the far end of the cloister and made out a denser patch of wavering shadow in the grey gloom. His heart seemed to leap into his throat. He couldn't swallow. He could hardly breathe.

A hooded monk-like figure was standing there, its hand on the head of an enormous wolf. Behind them, the rest of the demon wolf pack clustered, their glowing eyes fixed on Jonah. He froze to the spot. His legs seemed to have forgotten how to move. Slowly, silently, the wolves and the hooded shape approached.

With horror, Jonah realised that this was the whispering, faceless form of his nightmares, the robed shape he kept seeing. Under the hood, two yellow wolfish eyes gleamed out of blackness. As the shape moved, the folds of its robe flowed as if they covered nothing but shadows. Jonah backed against the pillar.

'What do you want?' he stammered.

A sound came from the figure, a gust of dirty air tainted with sulphur. Jonah recoiled, coughing. Then he began to make out words that seemed to whisper from an echoing cavern.

'I am here to claim you. You are to come with me to the Abyss.'

'No!' Jonah pressed himself against the pillar, his hands feeling for something he could cling onto.

The figure laughed and the sound echoed around the corridor. The wolves panted, locking their greedy eyes on Jonah, daring him to run.

'I am the Wolfmaster.' The whisper travelled around the cloister. 'In the Underworld, you will become what your destiny intends – the servant of the Black Lord of Komi. He desires the use of your gifts in his domains.'

'What gifts—?'

'The gift you have inherited from the Heart Eater. You will command the dragons at the Black Lord's bidding. Come.'

'No! I won't!' Jonah's voice rose to a shriek.

The Wolfmaster stepped closer until Jonah could see nothing but the blackness under his hood. This time the echoing voice pierced the gloom like a blade of ice.

'Do you think I and my wolves have scoured the earth for a thousand years and more to be denied now?' The rasping whisper rose in the sighing wind and reverberated around the stone walls. 'I have been tireless in my hunt for those with the gift of the dragon tongue. Many are the times that I endured cruel punishment when I failed to bring to my lord the prize of a Dragon Master.' The robe shivered and swirled. 'Then new word came of a boy whose ancestry might be revealed, if a Welsh dragon emerged from sleep. And, *at last*, the word was true.'

The figure made a throaty sound that Jonah supposed was laughter. As he turned his head away from the disgusting, rotting-egg smell of the Wolfmaster's breath, Jonah caught sight of a helmeted figure peering across the quadrangle from the cloister opposite. The person suddenly straightened up and abruptly disappeared into the darkness, re-appearing at a door that opened on to the lawn. It was Erin! And she seemed unhurt. Jonah could hardly believe his own eyes. She started to run across the grass.

Jonah was frantic. 'Erin! Go back. Go back!'

She hesitated. 'I mean it,' Jonah screamed. 'You can't help me. Run!'

Her hand flew to her mouth, as she realised that the wolves had found him. Then she turned and darted back into the corridor.

'Enough. It is time to leave Earth's surface,' said the Wolfmaster.

From somewhere deep inside, Jonah felt a knot of anger growing. He clenched his fists and stood up straight. Let the hooded nightmare cackle! He wouldn't sniffle like a little kid and meekly go to Hell with this stinking shadow and his demon wolves. They wouldn't take him down to the Abyss without a fight.

'Come,' ordered the Wolfmaster.

'Make me!' said Jonah.

The Wolfmaster's sulphurous breath made Jonah gag, as the shadowy figure laughed. He caressed the head of the dominant wolf.

'Give the boy to me,' breathed the Wolfmaster, and the animal demon lunged. Jonah kicked upwards as the wolf sprang, hitting its belly hard with the toe of his boot. It fell sideways, but one of its forefeet scraped Jonah's temple. Blood poured down his cheek. The other wolves fell on him, knocking him to the ground. They trampled over him, biting at his clothing and trying to rip it off. One was trying to get his helmet off by gripping it with its teeth. Above the snarls and yapping, Jonah became aware of a swishing sound and feet running down the corridor. Something landed with a thud near his head, and pandemonium broke out.

The wolves turned from Jonah to snap and growl at a new threat. The Wolfmaster howled in anger. Jonah raised his head and gasped as Erin, brandishing a huge sword in both hands, brought it down on a wolf's neck. The animal leaped away, squealing, and then shuddered and fell lifeless to the ground. A dark shape slid from its mouth and drifted up into the shadows. Erin whirled the sword again and rammed it under the forelegs of a wolf that was about to jump on her. It shrieked and limped away. The Wolfmaster's shadow curled round the walls.

'Jonah,' she yelled, as the wolves snarled round them. 'I brought a candle. Quick, light it. Do what Mike did. Hurry up!'

Jonah scrambled to his feet. The massive white altar candle was easy to see in the gloom but he couldn't find any matches.

'There by the pillar. To your left a bit!'

Erin backed in front of him, swinging the sword to hold off the wolves, while he dropped to his knees, feeling wildly round the pillar. His hand closed on the box she had thrown down. Jonah's fingers shook while he fumbled to take a match out and light it. The first one flared up and then died.

'Hell!' He tried again but the next one would not light. He could hear Erin grunting with effort as she whirled about, hacking at the snarling animals.

'Jona-a-ah!' Erin was panicking. She couldn't swing the heavy sword much longer.

The third match stayed alight. He held it to the candle, made sure the flame was burning steadily and then painfully scrabbled to his feet. A wolf jumped out of Erin's reach and leaped at him. He was knocked off his feet but managed to ram the flaming candle at its muzzle and, as it threw itself sideways, he swept the flame along its flanks. Immediately its coat caught fire and it fell heavily on top of Jonah, its hide blazing. With all his strength, Jonah heaved and pushed it off. The wolf, now a screaming fireball, ricocheted around the quadrangle until it fizzled upwards, like a firework, into the night sky.

Erin was flagging from the effort of holding the sword. She leaned against the pillar for a moment, panting for breath, while Jonah edged in front of her, still brandishing the candle at the wolf pack. Two more wolves dissolved into howling balls of flame, as Jonah swung the candle round, desperate to keep the creatures off. Erin raised the sword again.

'Let's finish them,' she said.

The children forced themselves to pace steadily, side by side, towards the Wolfmaster and the last three demon wolves. Growling horribly, the animals crouched, ready to spring.

Jonah suddenly remembered the charm paper in his pocket. He pulled it out.

'Say the spell!'

They walked determinedly forward, side by side, chanting loudly. Erin brandished the sword while Jonah's large white candle threw flickering shapes on the walls. The Wolfmaster, eyes blazing with rage, tried to reach out for the children, but the candle and the sword held him off. He lunged at the children again and again, but he couldn't reach them across the candle flame and the glow of the sword's blade. As they chanted, the Wolfmaster seemed to shrink. His wolves slunk behind him, whimpering.

As they saw the demons' power diminishing, Jonah and Erin's confidence grew. They kept advancing, holding the sword and the candle high. Then, quite suddenly, it was all over. The Wolfmaster's robe began to fold and slip towards the floor. A terrible, moaning wave of sound swept over the walls of the cloister and a dark, formless shape blew up towards the roof of the arcade, hovered for a moment by the stonework and then floated out of the cloister and up into the dark night.

When Jonah turned back to the wolves, they were nowhere to be seen. The hooded robe lay empty on the stones.

The children, gasping in lungfuls of air, stared at each other and lowered their weapons.

'They've gone,' Erin panted.

'Thanks to you. You saved my life! He was going to take me down to the Underworld. Erin, you were *fantastic*.' Jonah grinned at her as she propped the huge sword against the wall. 'Hey, where did you get that?'

'I was wondering where my sword went,' said a familiar voice, as Mike Golding came along the corridor towards them.

Chapter 26

JONAH SETS A CONDITION

Erin flushed as she lifted the sword and held it out to Mike. She bit her lip. 'I'm sorry. I know I shouldn't have touched it, but I didn't know what else to do.'

Jonah was open-mouthed. 'You're *sorry*? If it wasn't for you, I'd be dead by now.' He turned to Mike. 'You're not mad at her, are you? She totally saved my life. If she hadn't come back with your sword, that evil hoody-thing would have taken me down to Hell.'

Mike smiled at them both and patted Erin's shoulder. 'Of course I'm not mad with you. You seem to have been amazingly brave. Both of you.' He weighed the sword in his hand. 'I'm surprised you could lift it, Erin.'

She beamed up at him. 'I just had to. You can do – like – impossible things if you have to, can't you?'

'Certainly seems so.' Mike gave her a wink and turned to Jonah. 'What were you doing in the cloister?'

'The ape-gargoyle threw me off the roof.' Jonah explained what had happened after Ffyrnig had put him down in the quadrangle. 'I thought it might have killed you,' he said to Erin. 'How did you get off the roof? How did you find me?'

'Well, when you began to slide down, the ape was over the moon – it obviously thought you would be killed – and then, when Ffyrnig caught you, it started screeching and swearing. I was so scared! It watched Ffyrnig fly away with you and then it started coming back for me. All the other demons had been driven off by then, but two angels heard the noise it was making. Luckily for me they came to see what it was shrieking about and saw me lying there. Before the demon knew what was happening, one chopped its stone body in two – just with one swipe. It didn't stand a chance! And the other one carried me down on to the Green. He healed the demon's bites.' She laughed, and stretched gingerly. 'I bet I'll still have some lovely scrapes and bruises from being banged about on the roof, though. I'm starting to feel really sore.'

'But how did you know where to find me?' Jonah asked.

'The angels saw Ffyrnig fly behind the cathedral with you, so I started to look for you. And then, when I saw you in the cloisters with the wolves, I remembered Mike – erm – Saint Michael's sword —'

'Oh, not *Saint*,' Mike cut in. '"Michael", if you really must.'

'I'd noticed it lying on the altar steps, when I'd run up the nave to start looking for you.' She looked up at Mike. 'Did you put it there to kind of get its strength back?'

'Something like that,' Mike nodded.

'Anyway, I dashed back to get it, Michael, and I remembered how you used fire on the wolves in the valley, so I took an altar candle as well.' She blew her cheeks out. 'Our luck was really in, Jonah. If there hadn't been any matches near the candle-stand, we should only have had the sword.'

Jonah sighed. 'I can't believe it's all over.'

'Well, it is. And no small thanks to you two. You have been incredibly brave.' Mike put an arm round Jonah's shoulders. 'Come on. I believe there's some hot drinks and cake waiting for you two in the bishop's palace.'

They had just come into the bishop's sitting-room, when Bryn with Claire and Rhodri, Emlyn and Gwen were shown in.

'You're squashing me, Mam,' Erin giggled, as Gwen hugged her again and again. After the hugs and the exclamations had died down, the two families and the cathedral clergy, with a couple of police officers and two or three SAS officers, sat down to hot drinks, sausage rolls and cake. Jonah was ravenous but, at last, over his second hot chocolate, he and Erin started to tell the whole story of the awakening of the Last Great Dragon and the emergence of the demons. The adults kept exchanging glances and shaking their heads. 'Unbelievable,' they murmured.

The Dean of Hereford leaned towards Jonah. 'And who exactly was this Wolfmaster? He sounds like the essence of evil. Blood-chilling.'

'He was awful.' Erin shuddered.

'He said he had orders to find me,' Jonah said thoughtfully, 'And it sounded as if he had been looking for other boys like me – you know, descendants of Heart Eaters – for hundreds of years. He said his master wanted me to control other dragons for him.' He swivelled round to look at Mike. 'Who's the Black Lord? Because that's who I was supposed to work for.'

Mike shook his head.

'I don't know. Lots of evil spirits might call themselves that. Maybe I've heard of him under another name, but the Wolfmaster is a puzzle, I must admit. Still,' he smiled and looked round the room, 'they have gone and I doubt they will be back in Hereford. They know now that they cannot use the Great Dragon to frighten human beings, so I don't think you will have anything else to fear. Thanks to Jonah and Erin and Ffyrnig, you can all sleep well tonight – or what's left of it!'

'Ffyrnig!' Jonah jumped up. 'Oh, poor Ffyrnig. Where is he? I've got to go to him.'

'He's fine,' said the bishop's wife kindly. 'He's a wonderful beast, isn't he? He's having a meal on the lawn. Mr Parry – Rhodri, that is – only just got back from Credenhill barracks. He thought the dragon would be hungry, so he went to get some meat for him. Ffyrnig seems very content.'

Jonah's face lit up. 'Oh, thank you. That's really kind. Would it be all right if I went out to him?'

The bishop smiled. 'Of course. May I come with you and make his acquaintance?'

Jonah and the bishop strolled out into the palace garden. The sky was beginning to lighten.

'Nearly morning,' the bishop said. 'And the dawn of a much more hopeful day, thanks to you and Erin and the Last Great Dragon of Wales.'

Ffyrnig was lying under the trees, lazily licking at the last of his meat.

'I'll tell him you would like to meet him, shall I?' Jonah asked the bishop.

'Please. And say how grateful we all are.'

As they began to walk over to the dragon, Mike joined them. 'I must go now,' he said. 'But don't worry. We are always watching over you.'

Jonah had a sudden thought. 'Mike, can we use phones and the TV now? I'd love to phone my parents.'

Mike shook his head. 'Not yet, I'm afraid. The enchantment the demons placed on your communication systems will take a little while to lose its power. But with no evil spirits around to keep it strong, the systems should be back to normal in a few days.' He turned to the bishop and bowed his head. 'My Lord, I believe Hereford and the Radnor Forest are safe again.' Then he took Jonah's hand with a huge smile. 'Well done, you and Erin. Everyone is going to be very proud of you. In fact, I think that you and Erin and Ffyrnig are going to find yourselves pretty famous, when the radio and TV come back on.' He grinned. 'Be brave and put up with it!'

A light glowed round him. Jonah saw the outline of the Archangel's wings and the gleaming gold of his hair, and then Saint Michael had gone. The bishop drew a deep, tremulous breath.

'Shall we go to meet Ffyrnig?' Jonah asked quietly.

The bishop nodded and they walked over to the dragon, who was looking towards them eagerly.

'Ffyrnig, I have brought the Bishop of Hereford to meet you,' said Jonah.

As he hissed and crackled to translate what the man and the dragon said to each other, Jonah thought the bishop hid his amusement very well. Jonah told Ffyrnig what everyone had talked about in the palace.

'But even Saint Michael doesn't know who the Wolfmaster was,' he said. 'All we know is that he wanted to kidnap me for some Black Lord.'

Ffyrnig's eyes snapped open. 'Black Lord?'

'Yes. Do you know who he is? The Wolfmaster said he had been punished before now, because he couldn't produce someone who could talk to dragons.'

Ffyrnig puffed out a fiery breath. The bishop took a step backwards.

'Steady on, Ffyrnig. What's the matter?'

'Did the demon just talk about a Black Lord? It wasn't the Black Lord of Komi, was it?'

Jonah thought for a moment. 'I think that was the name. Yeah.' He turned to the bishop. 'Ffyrnig's saying he knows who wanted to kidnap me.' He looked at the dragon again. 'So where is this Komi?'

'It's a beautiful land in the North. They say there are forests, and many rivers, and many herds of reindeer. Good hunting for my kind.'

'Does this Black Lord rule the country then?'

Ffyrnig turned his head from side to side. 'No, he who calls himself the Black Lord of Komi is a dragon.'

'A dragon?' Jonah was astonished.

He explained to the bishop what Ffyrnig had just said. 'This is so weird,' he said to him. 'Why would a dragon actually spend years and years looking for someone who could control him?'

Ffyrnig was looking thoughtful. 'The Black Dragon of Komi is a Great Dragon, like me. I didn't know he was still on Earth, Master. Perhaps he wanted you to keep order among lesser dragons who might rebel against him. He's supposed to be a vicious creature. You must beware of him and his demon slaves.'

'Don't worry,' said Jonah, stroking the dragon's neck. 'The Night Creatures have gone and we've got the angels to watch out for us now. We're all safe, and you are going to be so famous! The whole world is going to want to visit you. We'll have to think of somewhere you can live, to get a bit of peace. Oh!' A thought struck him. A surprisingly unpleasant thought. 'You won't want to go down underneath the forest again, will you?'

Ffyrnig threw him a sideways glance. 'Would that not please you, Master? I'd be out of your way.'

'Oh, Ffyrnig. I don't want you out of the way. Erin and I would miss you so much. Can't you stay in the valley? Please!'

Jonah threw his arms round the dragon's neck and hugged him, while he told the bishop what they had been saying

Ffyrnig squeezed his eyes shut happily.

'Oh, Master, I should like that very much.'

'Wonderful! But, well, there is one condition.'

Ffyrnig looked at Jonah apprehensively. 'Master?'

'No more of that 'Master' stuff,' said Jonah firmly. 'We're friends. And we're partners. So this is the condition: you must never call me Master again. I'm Jonah to you.'

The Last Great Dragon screwed up his eyes with pleasure. 'Oh, Mas—Jonah! You don't know how happy you've made me.' He sighed with delight, and a shower of sparks, carried on his smoky breath, streaked up into the brightening sky.

OUR STREET
BOOKS

Our Street Books for children of all ages, deliver a potent mix of
fantastic, rip-roaring adventure and fantasy stories to excite the
imagination; spiritual fiction to help the mind and the heart
grow; humorous stories to make the funny bone grow; historical
tales to evolve interest; and all manner of subjects that stretch
imagination, grab attention, inform, inspire and keep the pages
turning. Our subjects include Non-fiction and Fiction, Fantasy
and Science Fiction, Religious, Spiritual, Historical, Adventure,
Social Issues, Humour, Folk Tales and more.